Dead Flowers
and other Stories

Derek Wynford Jones

OPENING CHAPTER

First published in 2014 by:
Opening Chapter, Cardiff

openingchapter.com

ISBN 10: 1-904958-52-4
ISBN 13: 978-1-904958-52-9

To her and him and them all (and the rest)

Introduction

An eclectic mix of stories old and new that offer unique insights into the lives, inner and outer, of some of the weird and wonderful human beings that inhabit this planet we call Earth in the early twenty-first century.

Some of the stories herein were originally published elsewhere, including in *The Walker and Other Stories by Derec Jones,* published in 2006, and in *For the Time Being by Derek Wynford Jones* published in 2014..

For this new collection, some of the older stories have been revisited and re-edited, and new stories have been added.

Derek Wynford Jones.

Contents

Dead Flowers

Twenty-seven people were killed or injured when the bomb exploded. I happened to be travelling past on the bus, but I was only shaken up a little.

I went to help of course; I am a doctor after all. I attended to three of the victims. Mair died on the spot and Alice lost a leg, but it was Keith who got my sympathy. I suppose it was because I identified with him more than I did with the others. He was a man, we were about the same age and more significantly, it had been twenty-seven years for me too.

Keith whispered: "Twenty-seven years married, I thought I'd seen it all," he laughed.

I laughed with him, there's not much else you can do in a situation like that. He wasn't seriously hurt in a physical way, but I could see the damage just as clearly as if he was. I knew the signs.

"I thought it couldn't get any worse, after I lost my job," he said quietly. "But of course it could, and of course it did."

"Don't worry, it won't be long now."

"I'm OK," he said. "There's no need to bother with me. Better go and see to the others, they need you more."

I looked around. Through the dust, everything was surprisingly still and quiet.

"Is Mair dead?" he asked.

He already knew. Her blood and pieces of her face were dripping off his arm.

I nodded.

"We had a good life, you know," he was smiling,

1

looking inward. "She always wanted to see a big London show, so we spent the last of my redundancy on tickets for tonight. This seemed like a nice little bar, so . . ."

A scream of pain pierced the stillness.

Keith raised his eyebrows "There's always someone worse off."

There was no need for me to go and help anyone else; there were so many police, paramedics and doctors on the scene by then that I was quite redundant, but I wanted to stay with Keith. It's the trauma and the shock you see, it can sneak up on you unexpectedly. You feel as if someone's hit you on the head with a sledgehammer. You can be so wrapped up in your own set of illusions about the world that you don't see it coming. Afterwards you feel very foolish, as if you've failed badly. The only way to cope is to blame yourself.

"I've really blown it now," he said. "She's gone and that's that."

Gradually the mess of bodies in the pub started to make sense. The shambles untangled and sanity returned as we adjusted to that terrible reality. Keith smiled and shook his head in wonderment at the cool professionalism of the emergency services.

"Nearly there," I said.

He nodded and looked around the mayhem, pausing only for a fraction of a second on the neat mantle of material that covered his wife's mangled body.

"Are you married?" he asked.

The more seriously injured had been ferried away

and the dead were covered up; Keith was next on the list. The investigators moved in as the paramedics lifted Keith into the ambulance. I went with him. He seemed pleased.

"I enjoyed our chat," he said, "it's not every day you have a real doctor all to yourself for so long."

"Me too."

I really had enjoyed being there with Keith in the worst circumstances imaginable. Two kindred spirits relaxing together, knowing that nothing worse could possibly happen, for a while at least.

"Mind you," he said, "I've done most of the talking, I don't know much about you. What sort of doctor are you anyway?"

"I'm a paediatrician," I replied.

"Sick children?"

"That's right," I said.

"I'd never be able to do that job," he shook his head. "Whatever made you want to become a doctor?"

"It's about putting something back, making a difference," I said.

"That's very admirable," he said.

"Not really, it's just something I had to do."

"What are those for?" he asked, indicating the battered bunch of flowers I was still grasping in my hand.

"Anniversary," I replied. "Twenty-seven years."

"Well, isn't that strange, same as me, though mine isn't until tomorrow. Well it would have been tomorrow," he sighed.

"You mentioned a son earlier," I said. "Do you want me to get in touch with him?"

"Aye, if you like, the number's in my diary, or on the mobile, but that was in Mair's bag. Have you got a phone?"

"Yes, where's the diary?"

"Here," he tried to reach into the pocket of the sports jacket he was wearing, but he didn't have the strength. "You get it," he said. "It's on the inside of the back cover, that's where I keep important numbers. It's under Gwynfor – that's his name, after his grandfather – Mair's father."

As I spoke into the phone, Keith stared at the inside wall of the ambulance.

"Was he there?" he asked, without looking away from the wall.

"Yes."

"That's a change, it's usually an answerphone. He's so busy. I wonder if he'll be able to get up to London."

"He said he would."

"Loved his mother, he did. Me and him though, we never got on. Looking back, I realise I was too overbearing, too protective. It's easy with hindsight though, isn't it? Have you got any kids?"

The ambulance stopped suddenly outside the hospital. I followed the trolley into the chaos.

While we waited for attention, Keith rambled: "Not long after the bomb went off I saw a man stumbling past, arms outstretched. He didn't have any fingers. Don't suppose he'll hold a pint for a while. Strange thing though, it seemed natural at the time."

"I'm not surprised," I said, "you can get used to anything."

"Yes, I suppose so, especially in your profession."

1

I nodded.

"You imagine all sorts of things," he said, "you know, when you see the news and all that, but it's not like you think it's going to be, at all. It's not so bad you know. It could be worse; at least I've had some sort of life with Mair."

A nurse came and took some details off Keith and a doctor gave him a good examination. When they left Keith drifted into a trance. He stared silently at the pastel colours of the hospital walls. I waited.

"How many died?" he asked eventually.

"Don't know," I said. "Seven or eight, I think."

"Oh!" he sighed. "It could have been worse, the place was packed."

"Yes," I said, "maximum effect, minimum risk, it's quite clever, it looks good on the news. It's a wonder it doesn't happen more often."

"Most people are decent," he said, "people like you and me, ordinary people, going about their daily lives."

"It only takes one or two," I said.

Keith nodded. He stayed silent for a long time after that. I didn't mind sitting with him. Gaynor would understand, and Matthew. At least they were together, I'd join them soon enough, there was no rush.

The pandemonium in the hospital settled down. Keith drifted off. I wanted to let him sleep; he looked so peaceful, as if he'd finally solved the puzzle of life, but a nurse came and woke him up; she was worried about concussion.

He saw me first. "Oh, it's you," he said drowsily,

"don't you have to be somewhere, your anniversary?"

"No, it can wait," I said. "I haven't missed one in twenty-seven years, there's plenty of time. They're not going anywhere."

"Your wife and children?"

"Child," I said, "just the one, a little boy."

"Just like me," he said. "Though Gwynfor's not so little now, big lump of a thing. Any sign of him yet, by the way? What time is it?"

"It's nearly midnight."

"You'll have to buy some fresh flowers," he said, shaking his head, "those are well and truly dead now."

I looked blankly at the flowers that I was still clutching and realised I'd probably killed them myself by holding them too tightly.

A nurse came over and explained that they had a bed waiting for Keith.

"I'd better go," I said. "Do you mind if I come and see you tomorrow?"

A tall young man rushed in and waited nervously for me to leave.

Keith managed to lift his hand. He squeezed my arm. "That would be great," he said.

I noticed tears forming in his eyes.

"You'll be all right," I said.

I dropped the dead lilies into a bin outside the hospital. It was already too late for the anniversary. In the taxi, I felt tears welling up in my own eyes for the first time in twenty-seven years. I was sure Gaynor and Matthew wouldn't mind if I skipped the anniversary. After all, it was more than a quarter of a century since I'd insisted on popping into the pub on the way home from the maternity ward. All I wanted was to show my new son off to my mates, I wasn't going to drink or anything. Then the bomb exploded, killing them both.

The taxi passed the cemetery on the way to my flat. I blew a kiss. "See you soon," I whispered.

How to Win the Lottery

Branwen's mobile phone shivered in her hand. It was Harry, her hyperactive younger brother. He was always a distraction. He could be a bit too much sometimes, but she was in a generous, and bored, mood.

"Are you in?" Harry said excitedly. "I'm outside – buzz me up."

Branwen obliged. One minute later Harry stumbled into the flat clutching his new laptop. Branwen was surprised. Harry's computer set-up in his own flat was usually untouchable, immovable, sacrosanct, with leads and dongles stuffed into every orifice. She only had to talk too loudly and he was on the ceiling.

"What's up bro?" Branwen asked.

Harry perched on the edge of the settee and put the laptop carefully on the coffee table. He flipped the lid open.

"Look," he said. "Come and see."

Branwen sat beside her brother and stared at the screen. There was a display of six coloured balls bouncing slowly at random. On each ball was a number.

"What is it?" she asked.

"Can't you see?" he said.

"It looks like a load of balls to me."

"Ha ha. Very funny – but honestly, can't you see what they are?"

Branwen shook her head. "Nope."

"It's tomorrow night's winning lottery numbers."

"But the numbers are changing."

"Well all right. They're not the actual numbers – not yet. The program is still running, it's going to take another twenty hours. It's analysing over a thousand complex spreadsheets."

Branwen laughed. "Idiot! You've gone over the top this time."

"No, listen. I've been working on it for months – years. I didn't have the computer power before, but this new set-up I've got is awesome."

"No one can predict the lottery, not even an awesome computer."

"You're wrong," Harry said. "Look, let me explain."

Branwen sighed. "Oh – all right, but let me open a bottle of wine. This could take some time."

Branwen sipped the wine absently while Harry rambled on in his entirely logical way.

"It's just mathematics, physics. It's all about action and reaction – one thing follows another, it's obvious. Can't you see? For example, every lottery ball is different. Yes, I know they're probably ultra careful to get each ball as identical to the next as possible, but no matter how hard they try, each ball will be totally unique, different, if only by a few nanograms – a few specks more dust on this one, and a variation in the specific weight of the inks or dyes in another – and that's not even taking account of the differences at the molecular level. Then, the other variables, like the ambient temperature, the humidity, the time of year, even variations in the radio signals that pass through the space – every one of them is different – but, get this, it's predictable. If you know all the variables, what state they start in, what forces are acting on them, and so on, you can predict exactly what will happen. You can predict the lottery numbers."

Branwen shook her head. "I can't even think long enough to consider all the variables. I mean just a few that have come to mind: the air pressure in the machine, the time it takes the announcer to tell some anecdote, the vibration of a passing aeroplane, the barking of a dog in the next street – it's impossible."

Harry stood up and gripped Branwen's shoulders. "Yes, I'm not stupid. I know that. But don't you get it? You don't need all that."

"I don't get it – no."

"How long has the lottery been going? I'll tell you, it's twenty years. That's a lot of data, a big sample, and that's all you need. All you've got to do is examine that data, and the patterns, there's always patterns, that's how we do things: build bridges, fly aeroplanes, cook food, don't you see – everything is done to a pattern, it has to be, otherwise it doesn't make sense – it has no use, in fact, something without a pattern is nothing – it doesn't exist. So, all you've got to do is find the pattern. The pattern has already worked out all the variables, it's in their nature, that's what they do – the patterns connect the dots – make things real.

Branwen screwed her eyes and stared suspiciously at her brother.

"I'm not going mad," he said. "I can prove it. I started by trying to connect the numbers drawn to the dates of the draws, you know, the day of the month, divided by the number of the month, plus the square root of the year divided by the recorded temperature at the time the lottery was drawn – that sort of thing, but it was too simple, so I carried on adding variables and formulae and applying them to the history of the numbers drawn. Slowly, patterns started to emerge. At first it was just one or two numbers – not much more probable than you'd get by chance. I tested that – there was a definite difference. Then I got three numbers, before it fell away to just one or two again, until I realised I hadn't taken the change in the hours of daylight into account – the sun is a very powerful variable. This went on for some time, and I added more and more important variables, until now there are more than a thousand. A few weeks ago I had enough confidence to actually run a real time prediction and buy a lottery ticket. I won a hundred and forty quid with four numbers – since then it's been three or four numbers every time. Look."

Harry pulled a crumpled bundle of lottery tickets from his pocket. "See, I haven't cashed them in yet. There's about six hundred quid there."

Branwen became increasingly astonished as Harry brought up each lottery result on the Lottery website and compared them to the tickets he had in his hands.

"Are you sure you didn't just buy loads of tickets and only kept the winning ones?"

"Don't be silly. That would have cost thousands. Do you know the odds of winning just twenty-five quid?"

Branwen nodded, she did. "But that's still a long way from getting all six," she said.

"Not as far away as you think. All I needed was to identify one or two more of the major variables – and I did – this week. The last one was the human population of the world at the instant the first number is drawn – to the nearest ten thousand, that's predictable as well, but it took a few days to sort that one out – and a very big spreadsheet. So that was it – Bingo! It's perfect. I checked back to the very first lottery – on the internet, it lists every number ever drawn. I ran my program and it came up with the right numbers every time, including the last draw's results. And the beauty is I don't need any more variables. The ones I've got are enough to establish the patterns. Can't you see? We're going to be millionaires."

"We?"

"Well of course Branwen, you and me, we're a team. I couldn't have done it without you."

"I did nothing."

"But you did, can't you see? You're a major variable in my life – after everything. Without you I wouldn't exist – my pattern would never have been. You made me."

"No I didn't."

"Not in that way – that's just physical. Can't you see? There's so much more than that to existence."

"Yes, all right."

"So, tomorrow, you go out and buy a ticket. I'll text you the numbers when my program has finished running. I'll get one as well."

"Why do we need two?"

"Ah! That's just in case someone else wins, then the share would be diluted with theirs. This way we get two bites. I know, I know, you're thinking why can't I predict whether someone else will choose the same numbers. Well I could of course, but then that would involve investigating a whole new set of variables – and that's going to take time. Eventually, I'm convinced I can speed up that process – until it could be done in an instant. In fact, eventually I'm sure I can find a pattern that fits everything, not just the lottery. It will predict the stock market, football games, Oscar winners, life expectancy, the lot. And if you can predict you can control. We can have it all Branwen. We can own the world. We will be immortal."

Branwen noticed a gleam in her brother's eyes, a gleam she'd never seen before, as if a dark brooding monster was lurking there, a timeless demon woken up, ready to inflict his terrible rule on the universe. She shuddered.

"What's up Branwen?" Harry looked concerned.

He was her little brother again. She shook herself. "Nothing, it's nothing. It's all a bit much, that's all. I don't know what to think."

"Can I stay here tonight?" Harry asked. "I can't possibly go home, and I know I won't sleep."

Branwen nodded. "Of course. You can sleep on the settee. She yawned. "I'd better get off to bed. The TV remote is on the coffee table – help yourself."

"I won't need that," Harry said. "I want to run a few last minute checks, make sure everything works as it should, there's a lot of numbers in those spreadsheets."

Branwen went to bed leaving Harry stuck to the screen, his fingers a blur against the keyboard. She fell asleep quickly and drifted into a concoction of weird dreams about Cleopatra and Darth Vader, about the planet covered in a pattern, like a giant's spider's web. She woke suddenly. It was dead quiet. She took her phone from the bedside table – 4:24.

Branwen crept to the toilet and afterwards looked in on Harry. He was curled on the settee in the foetal position, sucking his thumb in his sleep. Seeing him like that reminded her of the promises she'd made to her mother before she died. Harry was her precious little brother, he had no one else. She had to do what she had to do.

In the morning Harry made a great show of preparing breakfast in the small kitchen. All the clattering woke Branwen up. She waited patiently. She knew what was coming, even she could predict that.

A few minutes later the door to her bedroom creaked open slowly and Harry edged in carrying a tray. Branwen eyed him through her fingers as he hesitated, looking for a space to put the tray.

"Are you awake?" he whispered.

Branwen opened her eyes. "Good morning Sunshine," she said, a phrase she'd repeated almost every morning in the years after their mother's death and before Harry went to university. He'd looked so nervous that morning as she waved him away on the train. She'd gone home and cried for hours.

By the time Harry graduated, the house had been sold, raising enough money to buy a cosy modern flat each, half a mile apart; and enough in the bank to allow them an easy ride, for the first few years at least.

The tray contained, as usual, enough toast and marmalade to keep Paddington Bear happy for a month, and, as usual, Branwen ate it all, as Harry enthusiastically expounded his latest mathematical theories.

Eventually, stomach full of soggy bread, and head full of soggy words, Branwen got out of bed.

"I need to get ready," she said. "I have to be in work in an hour."

Harry laughed. "That's a bit pointless Sis. You're going to be a millionaire tonight."

"Of course," she said, "but still, I enjoy my job. Saturday is my favourite day – you meet so many interesting people, listen to their stories, make them feel good about themselves."

"It's just hairdressing," Harry said.

Branwen shook her head. "Nothing is just anything Harry. You should know that. We're all different, all unique."

"I guess so. Don't forget to get the lottery on the way home."

Branwen had a good day at work. She made the most of it, knowing that things were going to change dramatically. It was probably going to be her last day. On her way home she dutifully bought the lottery ticket using the numbers Harry had texted her. She crossed her fingers and mumbled a little prayer: *'Please God.'*

When she got in she found that Harry had been shopping. The coffee table was laden with his favourite snacks and crisps, items that she'd had to get to like too.

"There's a bottle of champagne in the fridge — for later — for when we win."

Harry punched the air with joy. "Yee-Hah."

"Here's the ticket," Branwen said, handing it to Harry.

"Great," he said. "Not long to go now, less than one hour."

Branwen steeled herself. She knew it was going to be a challenging time. This was a big one.

Harry didn't stop talking about what they were going to do afterwards. First — a holiday, somewhere quiet. He'd invest in the best computer money could buy — even if it cost a million it didn't matter. It would make them unimaginable billions.

Branwen nodded and fed him a stream of nibbles from the table, and cups of chamomile tea from the kitchen, while he chattered incessantly in the living room.

The moment came. Branwen sat next to Harry on the settee and put her arm around him, pulling him tightly, tears growing in her eyes. She took a deep breath and braced herself.

The first ball came out. It rolled into the tube, every turn taking forever. She gripped Harry more tightly.

T-W-E-N-T-Y-F-I-V-E the announcer said as if he was speaking underwater.

She looked at her ticket, she looked at the screen. She could feel Harry fidgeting, shaking, next to her. Twenty five was not one of the numbers they'd chosen.

The second number came out, the third. Not one of them matched their numbers.

Harry was shaking, gurgling, fitting. His eyes rolled back into his head.

Branwen held Harry's hand in the back of the ambulance. He'd been stabilised and was sleeping twitchily.

In the hospital, Branwen sat at his bedside, waiting for him to come round, she had to be there when he did. He'd need her more than ever.

She felt a little guilt, but she knew she'd done the right thing. She'd found the thousand spreadsheets while Harry was sleeping, sucking his thumb. She'd changed one number in one cell of one spreadsheet – she didn't know which one; and she didn't know if her actions had made any difference to the outcome, but she did know that it had been the right thing to do. In fact, considering all the variables, it was the only thing she could have done.

The Dreamer

The creature woke up; it was screaming silently, becoming aware that it existed as a presence inside its own skull. It was a bundle of bones, hanging with flesh.

Where am I? Who am I?

Ah! Yes. He was what was known as a man, on a planet known as Earth. A few hours earlier he'd lain on that bed next to a woman, a similar collection of flesh and bones. They'd been together, sharing their existence on that small blue planet for twenty-five of its years. His name was Ianto; her name was Siân.

She was lying next to him now, her flesh and bones covered with a smooth skin. He reached across under the bedclothes and stroked her thigh with his fingertips.

Ah! That was good, better, he felt better. Why had he been screaming? Was it another one of those dreams? What had it been about this time? Memories of those other worlds became so faint, so soon after waking. Seconds before, in the normal rush of time, he'd inhabited a universe subtly different to the one he'd just woken into. But it was a blur. In a distant part of his brain there was only a vague hint of that other existence, and that was fading fast.

Dreams were a mystery to him, and to every other inhabitant of the planet, as far as he knew. What was their purpose? They seemed so important, so ubiquitous, even when you couldn't remember them, yet no one knew what they were or what their function was. Sure there were theories and endless experiments – but still no one had a clue – did they?

Ianto sighed, reached across to the bedside table to pick up his phone. Siân mumbled from under the duvet. He didn't hear the words but he knew she was asking him what time it was – she always did.

He touched the phone's screen. "Six-forty-seven," he said.

"Shoot!" Siân said, ejecting herself instantly from the bed and trotting towards the door. Ianto laughed and tried to slap her bare backside as she sped past. She paused and looked back at him, her eyes glowering. Oops! But life was pretty good at the moment. He smiled as his head sank back into the pillows.

It was a corridor with doors on either side. Coming towards him was a big thick-set creature who filled the space from wall to wall and from floor to ceiling. The creature's features were hidden in its own shadow but there was a glint of cold dead eyes.

Ianto pushed the door to his left and stumbled into a room. It was a hotel room. There was a young woman with long white hair sitting naked on the edge of the bed; she was polishing a long silver rifle. She looked up as he came in, her eyes pools of fluid metallic grey, like mercury. She lifted the gun and pointed it at Ianto . . .

And,
Bang!

He was waking up.

"I'm off to work then. I'll see you later," Siân's

voice, hovering at the edge of his consciousness.

"Sorry. Yeah." He opened his eyes.

"And don't get too depressed today. Something will turn up," Siân said, leaning over and kissing him on the forehead.

Ianto reached out to touch her, but she was gone.

If it wasn't for the nag of his bulging bladder he would have snuggled up and gone to sleep again, but he padded, naked, to the bathroom to relieve himself. He yawned and went back to the bedroom; it was only half past seven. Why so early? Then he remembered she had to prepare for that interview.

He texted her. "Good luck today xxx."

He shrugged into his dressing gown and went downstairs to the kitchen.

Tea. It was always the first thing – tea and a smoke, while he checked his emails and Facebook and caught up with the news. There was a giant asteroid heading towards Earth apparently – everyone on Facebook was joking about it. The general consensus was that it would be a blessing if the Earth and everything on it was blown to smithereens; humankind was a filthy parasite blighting the planet and would most likely evolve to go out and infest the galaxy with its maleficent presence.

Twenty minutes later he had solidly and definitely become Ianto. Time to face the realities of the day. Siân was wrong – he wasn't depressed and he wasn't going to get depressed, he was thinking, planning, experiencing existence from a different perspective. Why did he have to conform to what so-called normal society expected? The Truth was, normality was a completely weird concept, totally abnormal if you like. What was so normal about wandering about a planet, a speck of space dust in an infinite universe, your awareness trapped inside a stinking bag of blood and bones, while all around you, other bags of blood and bones dressed themselves in bits of material collected from the environment and gave themselves labels and rewards for manipulating fellow bags of blood and bones to collect more materials from the environment to wear, or eat, or shelter in.

Nah – he wasn't depressed, he wasn't even unhappy.

So, he lay down on the sofa and clicked the television on, just to pass the time, to provide a background hum, while he thought about what he was going to do. He wasn't stupid, he knew he had to do something – even bags of blood and bones needed looking after – feeding, exercising, that sort of thing – and he wasn't just a bag of blood and bones was he? He also had an infinity within, an inner space just as vast as that outer space. His consciousness hovered in that sacred spot between the quantum and the universal. Nah – he definitely wasn't stupid.

It was a shard, a thin rocky outcrop, just wide enough to plant his feet on, and he was balancing on it. Below there was a bottomless void, above was an infinite darkness, and he was alone and falling . . . falling . . .

And,

Bang!

He was awake – It was the doorbell and the hard

knocking on the front door. And he stumbled along the passage, and the chubby, chirpy little man was handing him a brown box and asking him to squiggle on a small touch screen with a plastic stick.

The parcel was addressed to Siân in their daughter Josie's handwriting. Shit, it would be Siân's birthday the next day – and midsummer, always a special day.

Ianto washed his face and dressed. He reckoned he could spend about twenty quid on a present for Siân, as long as it showed he'd been thoughtful it would be OK, she wouldn't expect too much from him because of his circumstances.

The town centre was busy seeing as it was a Friday so Ianto kept his head down focusing on his destination. He wasn't a fan of busy commercial centres. He was heading for a quiet side street, to the Fairtrade shop. He bought a selection of dark chocolate and a birthday card handmade from giraffe dung by deaf African children – it was three pounds twenty-five, but Siân would like that.

He was over five quid under budget so he'd head for the big chain pub nearby, he could get two pints for a fiver there, then a nice walk home through the park and he'd knock up some pasta ready for Siân's return from work. He wondered how her interview had gone.

Facebook was going berserk when he got back in – apparently the asteroid thing really was serious. He checked the regular news sites – they were playing it down, some reassuring 'official' statements about the asteroid passing by harmlessly before midday the next day, which just happened to be the Summer Solstice of course – so that was handy for the other types of sites, the religious ones and the crazy conspiracy ones, who were babbling away in a frenzy of apocalyptic fervour.

The beer, he'd stretched it to three pints, took its effect, and he crashed out on the sofa again. There was plenty of time to make the pasta – it was only three o'clock.

The people had their backs to him but they were walking towards him – but they weren't moving – he wasn't moving.

The floor was moving, it was dissolving under his feet and he was shrinking, becoming sub-atomic, falling in between the molecules, swimming in light, gulping the light – balls of energy rushing towards him, sweeping through him. He was dead . . . dead . . .

And,

Bang!

The front door slammed. Siân was standing over him.

"Ianto, you moron. Have you been drinking again?"

Ianto was a little boy being chastised, full of guilt, nervous, defensive. He fell off the sofa.

"Sorry, sorry."

Then. No! Why should he feel like that? The world was going to end in less than twenty-four hours and she was just a bag of blood and bones like he was and she had no right to talk to him like that – no right.

"Bitch," he said. "You've got no right to talk to me like that – no right."

She looked shocked, startled at his outburst. Then a calm look came over her face.

She nodded. "Right, all right, you're right. I don't have the right, but I do have the right to tell you that that's it – it's finished, we're finished."

Now Ianto was shocked – puzzled. He stood up.

"I was going to make pasta," he said. "How did the interview go? Did you hear about the asteroid?"

She nodded. "I'm going out," she said. "I'm eating out. People from work. You can sleep in the other bedroom."

He sat down on the sofa and watched silently as she shed her raincoat and her work shoes.

"I'm going to have a bath," she said. "Do you need to use the bathroom first?"

He shook his head but urinated into the privet in the garden after she went upstairs. The sun illuminated the lawn and most of the vegetable patch – there were still a few hours of daylight left – midsummer – a magical midsummer's evening. Maybe the last one if that asteroid really was on its way.

He shook himself. Nah, he was getting silly – paranoid. Those websites were nonsense, there was always someone predicting the end of the world. He sat on the sun lounger and lay back, closing his eyes against the still strong light.

And there was a wide green field, with huge red daisies, and blue buttercups the size of dustbins. He realised he was dreaming, but the dream didn't end, and the colours pulsed menacingly, and he wasn't sure if he liked it – he was scared – it wasn't real, he knew it wasn't real, but it unsettled him and he wanted his own reality back, he wanted that solid certainty of who he was, what his life was all about, so he squeezed his eyes shut and commanded himself to wake up – wake up.

And he opened his eyes and he was awake – or was he? The bed was too big – huge, the size of a bus. He was still dreaming – it wasn't right. He squeezed his eyes again, and again, and each time he opened them there was a different reality – multiple realities and he realised it was up to him, he could choose his reality.

And then it was morning again and he was touching her thigh and she was asking the time and it was only six o'clock. He smiled and got up, kissing her on the forehead.

"I'll go and put the kettle on," he said. "I'll make the porridge too. You've got a tough day today – and it's your birthday tomorrow."

And Siân looked up at him from under the quilt with her beautiful smiley eyes.

"I love you," she said.

The Walker

I used to be like you, leaning on a counter of my shop and staring out of the window at me walking by. You were not normal – I was. I didn't see me in my eyes like you don't now. You will come to understand that we are one, one day. In your world where everything has a place, even me, I am the madman walking by, I am your future, you are mine. At the end of this street I will turn left and make my way home at last. I have thought it through; it is good again. I'll sleep tonight.

It is 7 am, I am awake, it is still good. Time for breakfast: a cup of tea and a couple of slices of toast. I slept last night for at least five hours – that is a good night, five blissful hours of unconsciousness. Today I'll walk to the shops again. I'll go in to that one near the station where they sell the strong smelling tobacco, and I'll ask the price of the chrome Zippo cigarette lighter in the window. I won't buy it of course, how can I? Besides – I don't smoke, any more. First stop – the bathroom – that's a satisfying piss, the first one of the day always is, that's when I really need to empty my bladder; no need to stand there and shake it about nonchalantly waiting. God – I hate public toilets, always some pratt trying to see over your shoulder, as if to compare dicks. Is it a natural consequence of man's evolution, to stand, shoulders rubbing, next to complete strangers and stare at pastel coloured walls, while down below, your urine and theirs mix together before rushing on a journey that ultimately leads to the ocean and complete amalgamation?

On to the kitchen: such a complicated sequence of

actions to co-ordinate this morning. Items required: tea bag, cup (must be clean), milk (must be fresh(ish)), sugar, kettle, kettle lead, water, bread (not too stale), margarine, grill, peanut butter, jam, big plate, small plate, butter (or margarine) knife, another knife for peanut butter, yet another for jam, tea spoon. Will the toast burn while I'm washing the knives? What now? Turn the grill off. Shit! It's all getting cold. Radio on, get something to read – what's this? Last week's free paper – that'll do.

Chomp, chomp, delicious. *'Test Drive the New Rover'. 'First team lose by two goals.' 'Gang of shoplifters hit town.'* That's an interesting headline. *'Gangs of professional shoplifters are targeting stores in the town centre.'* Read on. Bullshit! Sensationalism! We're all alone really. No such thing as a gang. Christmas soon – the adverts tell me, I like Christmas; more people about and the shopkeepers are too busy to notice me; I can just walk all day – walk and observe, watch you in your hamster cages.

There's sly Ron in his China shop, no more than fifteen feet square. He's beady-eyed and friendly, too friendly? Is his name really Ron? That's what it says above the door – 'Ron's Best China'. Been there years, chatting up the customers, selling cheap china. Ron has got good bladder control, like the other small shopkeepers and stallholders in the market. No private toilets for them, they have to use the public ones when there's a break in custom. Like colourful coffins these shops and stalls, a fine place to spend the waking death of your middle years.

Me? I'm just a walker, a walker and a watcher. I observe, I see things and I interpret them in my head. It used to be just a game, when I was younger, playing with people's lives, my mind; but there's a price to pay. Open yourself up; peel away the layers of self-justification and stare at the void. The price of being different, of being aware. So, I walk, and watch, and remember, storing away all the looks on your faces. I spend many a happy hour lying sleeplessly in my bed thinking of you, recalling those expressions.

Can you picture this?

A body walks down a street or in a shopping arcade – a market. It's a man, could be a woman? Or maybe women are different. Does it have to be a man? This guy is walking. OK – you listening? He has his hands in his pockets, his head bowed, bent towards his feet – walking – he passes a shop window; you stare out from behind the counter. He lifts his head from the floor and turns it towards you. You expect an intelligent stare – an inner knowing glow – at least a mad look, something to make you shiver with unknowing. No, what you see is a blank frightened look – the face of a loser – a shambolic dirty-coated greasy-haired, pimply-skinned loser. He puts his head down and moves on, shuffling forlornly, in character, on the damp concrete floor. You sigh with relief and turn back to your life, your own hope renewed.

I'm still walking and watching.

Where was I? Sorry I have been walking and watching again, lost track of what I was telling you.

Yes, I'm walking and watching; past the new ethnic clothes shop at the end of the arcade. Bright enthusiastic young woman, hand written signs in black felt pen. I know the pattern: borrow a couple of thousand from the bank or from a yet-to-be-disillusioned relative for the sparkling new business venture. Choose a snazzy name – *Shine Shoes* or *Peter's Pots* or, as in the case of the ethnic clothes shop – *Global Village Fashions*. Imagine a chain of colourful shops in every high street in the land, the headlines in the financial sections of the quality papers: *'GV Fashions goes public'. 'GV's founder worth a hundred million.'* Imagine being invited to appear on panel games on the television and one day being privileged and respected enough to choose your *Desert Island Discs* on Radio 4, and your luxury item, what would that be? Go on, think about it, it's going to happen one day. The Businesswoman (or man) of the Year awards, live from the Savoy. Then the realities, slowly you begin to understand why the shop premises remained empty for so long before you eagerly snapped it up. Sitting behind the glass counter filled with pretty beads and nodding off, waiting for customers to arrive. Leaping for the phone to find that it is just another advertising salesgirl trying to sell you space in some special feature that the local paper is running about *'New Ethnic Clothes Shops at the end of Arcades' phenomena'* for half their normal rates. Bigger overdrafts, more borrowing, less income, more stress until one of two outcomes occurs. 1. Go out of business: either – quietly with an orderly winding up and closing down sale, or more spectacularly, in a bankrupt chaos. 2. Stay behind the counter – earning a consistently below average income

– drifting into middle age and then retirement, taking a fortnight's holiday each year. Biting your nails down to the quick worrying whether the temporary help you've taken on (usually a friend or relative) is ripping you off or losing your best customers. To be fair there are many other outcomes that may occur but based on the evidence that I have so laboriously gathered over years of walking and watching the above two are the most likely by far.

How do I a humble walker perceive these things? I too, once lived a copy of your life, I was one of you and I will be again. I will exchange glances with you; maybe I'll even exchange lives. Who knows?

I'm passing the pub now. The trendy, garishly-painted one with the extensively renovated interior, not that I've been inside, not my scene; but I have seen the adverts and caught glimpses through the windows. Bloody fortune spent on it over the last five years but it was worth it wasn't it? You, the landlord, about my age, I knew you once – lad about town, painted the bumfluff above your lip with your sister's mascara to impress the girls (or the boys?). There you are now, stretching and yawning in the late morning light, tidying up your bins. A thousand lungfuls of burnt cigarette ash and a hundred sodden, torn, beer mats – it must have been a good night? You're still not sure of your sexuality but you soldier on, the air is chilly in the side street next to the pub; never mind, give a shrug, get ready for the lunchtime rush, Barbados in the summer.

Old Fred in the corner shop, I see you too. You've seen it all you have, your shoulders tell it. And you say it often enough: *"I've seen it all"*. There: in your general grocer's sell-anything-if-it-sells completely unprincipled shop, a dying breed, soon to retire taking your cutting wit and sour face out of the public eye. Will you shutter up your windows and eventually sell up and buy a little bungalow to sigh your way to the grave in? Perhaps you'll don a dhoti and sit in the Town Hall Square doling out your wisdom to aspiring passing entrepreneurs for the price of a cup of tea? What will you do with your time now Fred? Who will you moan to?

Now that's interesting I wondered what was going to open up there. Empty for nearly a year that shop's been; used to be an Italian run greasy spoon cafe: they sold the usual British excuse for food, egg and chips, massacred cow in fibreless pastry with a tasty gravy – that sort of thing, washed down with sickly weak tea. If you read the menu properly and accidentally asked for pizza one day then the owner himself would come, flouncing out of the kitchen with your order proudly displayed on a large cheap white plate. Paulo made the pizzas personally; they were a work of art, a delight to eat, once discovered, hard to resist. Then the place suddenly closed, no warning, no signs of demise – a family argument some said. Now it's going to be another branch of an estate agency. Why is it when all around businesses are collapsing in the recession the estate agents are all opening sparkling new branches and renovating the old ones at great expense? The most expensive furniture, displays, glass, carpets and huge mature potted plants; there's more money invested in the reception area of a provincial estate agency than there is in most small companies. Whose money?

I walked these streets ten years ago. Where did they go, those ten years? Some things have changed, in fact everything has changed, yet nothing changes. I have my memories of those ten years and the ones before. Not much has happened, yet I have these memories. Are they really my memories? Or are they the memories of the head I inhabit? Have I always lived here? Looked out of these myopic eyes? Touched with these nail-bitten fingers? Or am I just for this billionth of a nanosecond, conscious of this life, with its memories, its pain and its potential futures? I can't remember anything else so I suppose this must be it – my life. How's yours? No, don't tell me, I know, or I will know, or I did know, anyway, somewhere in time and space, there is knowledge.

Do you know how many bytes it takes to make a gigabyte? A giga I suppose, or is that like saying it takes a camel to make a camelhair coat? Or a mole to make a molehill? Or a delivery to make a delivery-man? But what's a giga? I'm standing outside *'The Computer Shop'*, emblazoned on the window, in fluorescent green vinyl, it says: *'Now with 8 Giga-bytes of memory'*. I'll go in and ask the pretty girl sitting at the desk, looking intelligent. I go in, "What's a giga?" I ask. She looks at me distastefully. Sorry, I'm not in the shop, didn't have the guts. I'm not asking the question. She's looking at me through the window, hoping I'll go away; I'm not exactly high tech. I move on.

I like the Asian supermarket. The proprietor is a

large golden-faced man who smiles, even at me. I can wander around and pick up the goods I like and then pay for them without having to say a word. It's not the same as the large supermarkets, there's no pushing and shoving at the checkouts and somehow a minor eccentric like me is expected to haunt such places as this. There is no expectation of verbal communication, not like the bakers, where pointing is not enough, everything is so close together, you have to spell out your requirements, too much crammed into the same space and all of it unreachable except by the assistant.

I've dubbed myself the Walker; not just *a* walker, but *'The Walker'*. Do you like it? I've decided that I make you feel uneasy, I make you nervous. That gives me a presence, a personality, a purpose, power. It allays the sadness a little. How do you allay yours? I've come around the circuit; I'm looking at you again through the window of your shop; staring at you leaning on your counter. You're not aware of me yet. Here it comes, the glance, you can feel my eyes, you turn your head and our eyes meet.

You make me nervous. I feel uneasy. Why do you do that? Why do you always stand and stare into my shop like that? Who are you? Where are you going? Do you know that I've given you a name? *'The Walker'*. Good isn't it? Now piss off and let me get on with serving my customers.

Breaking the Rules

Wednesday night: I met this fit girl in the pub; we exchanged phone numbers. I wrote hers on a pack of silver Rizla cigarette papers. I don't want to appear too keen – treat 'em mean and all that, so I had an idea. There's fifty papers in the packet. I've decided that if she hasn't contacted me by the time I've used the last paper, I'll give her a call. Thing is, the pack is just about full, and because I only smoke about ten a day, that's an excruciating five days to wait.

I could cheat. I could smoke more; perhaps if I upped the stakes to twenty a day that would halve the time, or, if I offered the papers around, maybe when the guys are rolling spliffs – that would see them disappear in a night. I'm in a quandary. I always play these little games according to the rules, and the rules are quite clear – I have to wait until I've used all the papers in a legitimate way, and for the purposes of this game, the legitimate way is to carry on as usual and smoke the ten a day.

Oh my god, I've just remembered, I'm in the middle of another little game, I've promised myself I'll stop smoking by tea-time on Thursday. I'm stuffed.

Thursday morning: It's OK; I'll probably fail in my attempt to give up smoking anyway. I haven't succeeded yet and I've tried often enough. But, I've got to try; otherwise it wouldn't be playing the game. I feel better now.

Thursday night: Ten o'clock. I came home early from

the pub. I haven't smoked since teatime, but I've got no cigarette papers left. Thing is, there are rules to these games. One of the rules is that any new game overrides the rules of any old game, as long as it's a spontaneous new game, suggested by someone else.

We played that game in the pub, the one where somebody writes the name of a famous person on a Rizla and sticks it on your forehead. Then you have to guess who you are. I didn't volunteer the papers; it was Martyn who asked for them, he knows I smoke roll-ups.

It didn't take long for the papers to run out. I was Freddie Mercury at first; I didn't get it for ages; that was fun, but I'm not gay or even bisexual. Then Martyn went into a sulk because I made him Pavarotti; he can't sing, but he is a bit tubby.

Friday morning: Even though it would have been within the rules it felt like cheating so I didn't phone her. I haven't bothered going to work either. I get like that some days; I hate work, it's a boring, pointless thing to do with your time. I suppose it's all right if you love your job, or if you'd be dead lonely otherwise, but it's not for me.

Martyn loves work. He only lives a twenty minute walk away from the park where he works as a groundsman. He doesn't seem to regard it as work at all, it's more like a place he goes to warm himself up for the pub in the night, that's a twenty minute walk in the other direction, he's got it sussed all right.

Gary now, another one of the guys in the pub, doesn't believe in work at all. He says there's too much work in the world, everyone zooming about, creating greenhouse gases, destroying the planet. He thinks he's doing us all a favour by not working, helping to save the world. Thing is, he's always broke, always on the scrounge.

Friday night: It's late, gone midnight. No pub tonight. Gary and Martyn came round for a few spliffs and a couple of beers. We had a laugh, even when Gary and Martyn argued about work. Then Gary pointed out that it was him who supplied all the weed. That's one thing Gary does well, grow his own organic Welsh skunk. We all fell about laughing then, as you do. I'm knackered.

Saturday afternoon: I'll have to phone her soon.

Saturday evening: I'm buggered. I wasted an hour searching for the Rizla packet. Some silly sod must have used it to make roaches for the spliffs last night, and the leftovers have been flushed. I don't know if I care anymore though; but if she phones me first I'll have to go out with her, that's another rule.

I wish I could be like Martyn, or even Gary; they've both got it sussed in their own way. Me, I don't know what I want. I don't suppose she'll phone now, probably thinks I'm a little shit. I think I'll go to the pub. Gary and Martyn will have to meet me there if I phone them, that's another one of our games.

Saturday, late night: I had a long chat with Martyn in the pub. Gary didn't turn up, probably too stoned or something, he's always breaking the rules. Martyn's really cool; he's got something special about him. He's just simply alive; he shines like he's lit up inside.

Sunday afternoon: Martyn's dead. Gary phoned. Martyn was on his way home from the pub and some fucking joy-rider smeared him all over a bus-shelter. Gutted.

Sunday night: She phoned me. I couldn't be bothered. She wasn't that fit anyway.

Fuck the rules.

Captive

"This too must pass." These words have helped me in my long ordeal. They ring in my head like a mantra almost every minute that I'm stuck here in this God-forsaken pit of a room. If I divide the days into hours and the hours into minutes and the minutes into seconds and think only of the infinitesimally small time-period that I am conscious of now, it is just bearable; in fact it becomes like any other moment in my reality – never-ending and entirely ephemeral.

Those times that I come face to face with my captors are the worst – and the best. I crave for their presence to confirm my own existence. I despise their arrogance, that they have the power to liberate me, and the power to end my life; they are my Gods. There's the big one with the slow voice and hairy scarred hands, 'LOVE' it says in scruffy blue letters across one set of knuckles and 'HATE' it says in thick blood-red on the other.

He seems nervous today, there's a change in the atmosphere. Instead of shoving the filthy bowl of filthy food at me and hurriedly exiting – he lingers, as if he needs to talk. Now, I have the power. I hold the bowl jealously close, pluck out the food and cram it in my mouth. I pause, gagging on a piece of what smells like raw, rotten fish, but I force it down; I must live. I grunt at him, or at the nervous eyes visible through the narrow slits in his black balaclava.

"You all right?" he asks, hoping for the usual subservient nod.

I can't acquiesce today. Somewhere inside me, a

small vestige of human spirit bursts into flame. I don't care if he uses those bloody *"HATE"* knuckles on me again; I don't care if they throw away the key and leave me to starve with the rats. A deep energy flows into my limbs and I'm up, spitting out the garbage from my mouth. *When I get out,* I think, *I'll never touch fish again.* Mentally, I add this promise to the all the other hundreds of vows that begin with *When I get out . . .* even as I find my voice and scream at him with such force that he is thrown physically backwards.

"No!" I scream, "No! No! No! No! I'm not all right, you, you, you utter moron."

He stops his involuntary backward movement and stands still and immovable, his eyes tinged with angry red. I am drained, defeated. I fall to the cold, filthy floor at his feet. I am sobbing, crying uncontrollably. Through my tears I look up and see his muscled shoulders relax, his fists unclench. He turns and leaves without a word and I hear the heavy door clanging shut.

Darkness again; darkness where I scrabble about on the floor, feeling with my numbed fingers for the food that I have so carelessly scattered. It's a race between me and the rats. I am a rat. Soon, when I have crawled back to the stinking mattress, I fall into a crazed sleep. I dream.

I am nowhere; it is the end of the world, the end of time. I look this way and that, I see faces: my benevolent grey-haired primary school teacher, the dear old lady who wanted me to become a barrister, a politician, even Prime Minister. She believed in me once, now she stares at me in anguish. My dear husband, John, as a young man: no grey hairs, no deeply wrinkled face, no pot belly. He's crying. He can't see me. He's lost in the dark. My beautiful son, Adam, grown into a cynical man, smiling at me in a sickly patronising way. I can't go on. I want to die.

Thank God – it's a dream, I realise, it's not Apocalypse, it's now, I am alive; there is hope. My eyes are used to the dark again; you see it's not total. I smile at the shadows of the rats in the corners of my prison; they don't give up, this is their life. I am a rat. God how I love these creatures, my brothers and my sisters. Am I cracking up? Have I gone mad?

Something has woken me; I hear their voices, the bass tones of the big one penetrating the solid door, and the high pitch of the man I have come to think of as the 'Weasel', which sounds like the squeals of the rats. The door opens again and he comes in furtively, inching carefully over the threshold as if he is trying to avoid disturbing me. He is clever this one, clever like a small carnivorous animal of the woods. He is careful to put his black mask on before he enters but I can see those sly features clearly: the small pointed nose, the black marbles of his eyes flicking quickly from side to side, the greasy dark hair – hopelessly out of fashion, and the big uneven teeth. I could pick him out of an identity parade if I was blindfolded.

Weasel peers at me while his eyes adjust to the gloom, he disguises his voice as he speaks. So there is still hope, they don't want to be recognised. I will not die – yet.

"Are you all right?" asks Weasel, his voice coloured

with fear. He thinks that the big man has harmed me.

He will not beat me. He will not see my despair. "Yes, yes, yes I'm fine, I'm OK, I'm all right," I say quietly, but with strength.

Weasel sighs relieved and backs out of the door closing it gently. I wait for the sound of the bolts to signal that I am safe again, secure in my foetid womb where I can relax and indulge in my nightmares. All is silent, quiet minutes pass. *They've forgotten*, I think, *forgotten to bolt the door. No!* the inner voice says, *they are waiting outside with baseball bats, waiting for me to poke my head out like an impatient rabbit, waiting to club me into the bliss of death.* I cower in my corner for ever. *No!* I must conquer this apathy. *This too must pass*, and it will pass one way or another, it must end, in death or in liberty. Somehow emboldened, I don't care. I roll off the mattress, stand up and reach for the door; it's not locked.

I stagger out, no bats, no weasels, no HATE knuckles. It's an abandoned factory of some sort, the light beams through the broken roof and picks out my starved eyes, blinding me for a few moments. The floor is covered with old bits of metal and splintered wood. I tiptoe across towards a large opening I see on the far side.

Wait! What do I look like? Is there a mirror? A bathroom perhaps? Even a dirty puddle? I can't let John and Adam see me like this. What will they think of me? Perhaps I can get home without any fuss, slip in quietly and have a long hot bath before I have to face the world. I look down, my feet are bleeding, where are my shoes? My legs are bare, the designer skirt I bought to brighten up my life when I met the first hot flushes of the menopause has held up well. It's charcoal grey, it's absorbed the dirt well, it's in good condition; it should be, it cost over two hundred pounds, nearly all the cash I'd surreptitiously saved from the housekeeping. Why me? Why should they want to lock me away in that place? All I've ever done is look after my husband and my son; fed them, wiped the blood off their cuts and washed their smelly underpants.

I lurch outside into the full light of a warm spring; I appear to be on a derelict industrial estate. The grass verge next to the road is overgrown; it smells fresh and sweet as I fall down and feel myself losing consciousness.

~

The hospital staff treated me very gently and cautiously and kept mumbling about *Post Traumatic Stress Disorder* and counselling, but I was all right. They caught the men who'd held me, a couple of small time gangsters. They'd owned a small gymnasium, their business had collapsed. They were looking for an easy way to make fifty thousand pounds. John had always been a show-off around town, bragging about how well his motor-parts' business was doing and driving expensive cars. My captors hadn't realised that it was all a front. John didn't pay the ransom, the police advised him not to; he couldn't have paid it anyway.

The court case fascinated me, but it made me sad to see those two healthy young men get sent to prison for such a long time. After all what had they done that was so bad? At least I didn't have to wash their dirty underpants. Before they were sent down I edged as close as I could to them and told them I'd forgiven them. They seemed perplexed. Weasel looked just as I'd imagined him, but Knuckles was gentler, younger, frightened – like a child who'd lost his mother.

~

Now, I'm sitting at the breakfast table, back in my lovely house. John and Adam are still fussing over me, making sympathetic noises and asking me if I'm all right. "Are you all right, Mum?", "Are you all right Jane?" they ask. I just look at them and smile, "Of course," I say, "of course I'm all right."

I feel sorry for John, he's gone to look so old and grey, and fat; he's got nothing left. I can't forgive Adam for that cynical sneering look he gave me in my darkest moment, but I'm all right, quite happy really, and of course Monday is still laundry day.

Born to Lose

Walter? What sort of a name was that to give to a child born in 1995? Walter Andrew Nankeville. You don't need much imagination to know what nickname he acquired in later life. To be fair his parents were decent sorts, hard working and honest, and they only wanted the best for their one, and as it turned out, only child. Walter was quite happy in the nursery and infants' schools and for the first few days of the primary school. Then the naturally cruel older boys, as soon as they found out his full name, gave him the nickname that from then on moulded his character and his attitudes to life.

When he was just eight years old he decided that he hated his parents and never spoke to them willingly again. They, poor innocent souls, never understood why they had bred such an ungrateful surly child, even until the day they both died in a pointless car accident when Walter was a broody fifteen. His feeble parents, pathetic even in the method of their demise, skidded on a patch of spilt butterfat and ended up upside down, skulls shattered, on the concrete forecourt of a Lada garage.

By then he'd already become entrenched as a true loner. All around him his peers joined football teams, went to the cinema, and started on the painful adolescent discovery of sex. Walter kept his own company, and, to the other teenagers at his school, seemed to live up to his nickname. Walter developed passions of course; he collected things, coins, stamps, and the addresses of pen-friends he never wrote to.

In the summer after the death of his parents, the children's home that had taken him in sponsored him on a holiday to Wales. Walter didn't mind being sent to Wales, he wouldn't have minded staying in his room at the home either. Unfortunately, one of the staff at the adventure centre, some sort of patron saint of lost causes, decided to take on the challenge of Walter's lethargy and apparent disinterest, and made it her task to get him out of bed in the morning and push him into some sort of activity.

Walter realised that he had to do something with his body while his inner self brooded its way through his earthly existence so he didn't even mind that. He elected to go walking around the hills near the reservoir, on his own of course. Betty, his motivator, was not very happy at the prospect of Walter making the solo trek, but, she reasoned, it was better than him lying in bed all day and it might at last provide the trigger that would begin the process of him recovering from the tragedy of his parents' deaths.

Walter needed a rest, he'd been walking for over two hours, so he sat down on the banks of the reservoir and idly consumed the salad sandwich Betty had insisted he take with him. He heard the sounds of banal immature voices coming closer to his position on the bank; he looked up as two boys of about his age came into view through the trees. He'd seen them hanging about in the centre, a pair of city troublemakers, ignorant and noisy. Walter tried to ignore them.

"Hello mate," said the biggest, hair shaved almost to the bone, scarred face, cigarette between his fingers.

The two boys sat down, one each side of Walter. Walter grunted and continued to eat the sandwich self-consciously.

"Where's your manners boy?" said the second, a small ugly boy, as he reached across Walter to take the stump of the cigarette offered by the other. "Oops, sorry," he said, knocking the sandwich out of Walter's hands, scattering slices of tomato and thin stalks of cress over the ground.

Walter shrugged, tossed the remains of the sandwich to the fishes and stood up.

The first boy grabbed Walter's legs and pulled him back down.

"Going already? Stay here and have a fag with us."

Walter stood up again, mumbling "Don't smoke, got to go."

"Oh no you don't."

The two boys grabbed Walter and pulled him down again. Walter slipped on the damp grass, fell down the bank and into the shallows of the reservoir. The boys laughed at Walter's spluttering; they were still laughing as they went out of sight down the path. Walter struggled out of the water and sat heavily on the grass.

'So what?' he thought. 'Now I can go back to the centre and get changed, perhaps Betty will leave me alone at last.'

"Are you all right?" a deep Welsh voice came at him from above.

Walter looked up. At the top of the bank stood an older boy, almost a man really, with a concerned expression on his ruddy face.

"Yes. Yes. I'm fine, thanks."

"I saw you crawl out of the water; your two friends weren't much help, they've legged it now mun. How far have you come?"

"I'm staying at the activity centre, on holiday."

"I see. I know it, it's quite a long way from here, you'll catch your death walking back in that state."

"It's all right thanks," Walter said.

"No, wouldn't hear of it, you must come back to the farmhouse with me, it's only up there mun." The older boy pointed through a gap in the trees where the ground rose steeply.

Why not, Walter thought.

The farmyard and the stone-built house were a revelation to Walter. New sights, sounds, and smells bombarded his senses. A boisterous border collie bounded towards them, yapping excitedly. Agitated chickens scattered in its path, the flap of their wings throwing up the scents of decomposing vegetables and wet manure. The Welsh boy and Walter strode up to what must have been the front door of the house – a rectangle of blue flaking paint, the wood old yet solid. A narrow hall, barely carpeted, contained several pairs of wellington boots, a small table, and a middle-aged woman speaking into a phone.

The woman looked at them and nodded into the mouthpiece. "Yes, of course, look sorry bach, I've got to go, Dafydd's just come in, looks like he needs a bit of maldod, talk to you later, so-long te."

She hung up and turned to the boys: "You gone and fished another one out of the Llyn then Dafydd, what's the story this time? Who's your friend?"

"Dunno yet Mam, can we get him dried out?"

"Righto, you put the kettle on, I'll dig up some of your old clothes. Come here boyo, into the kitchen where it's warm. What's your name?"

Walter hesitated; his name wasn't something he shared willingly. He felt an un-experienced warmth in the house, an instant feeling of belonging – why not, new experiences, new people, new name. "It's Andrew," he said, "Andrew De Ville."

"Andrew, that's a good name, De Ville? Sounds foreign."

"Yes, my grandmo..., er grandfather came from France, Brittany."

"You're a fellow Celt then, we'll have to look after you now. Sit down, I'll fetch those dry clothes."

Walter liked the sound of his new name, it had a sophisticated sound; he repeated it silently to himself. Andrew De Ville, Andrew De Ville. . . How was it spelled? It would be two words, that surname. De followed by a space then Ville like the French for town. He'd learned that much at least in the years of French lessons he'd endured. School hadn't been a complete waste of time after all.

"Can you speak French then Andrew?" asked Dafydd as he poured the boiling water over the tea bags and set the aluminium teapot near the hotplate of the Aga to brew.

"Er, no, my father did, before, before he died, but I was too young to remember much."

"Did you say your father died?" It was Dafydd's mother coming back into the room. "You poor boy.

How did your mother cope?"

"I'm afraid that they both died. I was very young; they were both journalists, in some place in Africa. They got attacked by rebels. I was lucky, apparently I slept through it all, they found me the next day and I was brought back to Britain to live with my grandmother."

Dafydd and his mother opened their mouths in shock and shook their heads in sympathy. Walter paused, God they were lapping it up, eager for more.

"My Gran, she's a retired musician, used to be a ballet dancer, looked after me for years. She's not very well now, can't cope like she used to, so I came on this holiday to give her a break more than me. One of her nephews, a sort of uncle to me suggested it; he's got some shares in the centre I think. He said it would help me to see a bit of life before I concentrate on my A levels next year."

"Duw, Duw," said Dafydd's mother. "You have found a live one this time Dafydd. Look at me, so rude. I'm Mrs Grufydd, pleased to meet you Andrew. Now then, take these clothes, you can go and change in the parlour, show him where it is Dafydd."

Walter was ushered in to the parlour, a pristine room with polished dust-free sideboard and floral patterned three-piece suite. Crocheted circles perched precariously on the back of the chairs so that Walter was afraid to sit down on them. Dafydd closed the door on Walter and after a few minutes alone Andrew emerged dressed in Dafydd's best old clothes.

Andrew De Ville was born, he felt the joy of living, he was confident, intelligent and capable. He returned to the kitchen. Soon the two Gruffydd's were laughing and marvelling at Andrew's memories of life with his Gran in her Chelsea apartments and the rich characters she socialised with.

"Well I never knew that, all those Lords and Ladies could behave like that, just goes to show. Now, Andrew will you stay to tea?"

Andrew wanted to agree but Walter mumbled something about having to get back and perhaps he could call again if it was all right. Mrs Grufydd had a very efficient tumble drier and she even gave the dried clothes a bit of a going over with her steam iron before returning them to Walter.

Dafydd walked with Andrew back to the path around the reservoir. Before they parted Dafydd sighed. "How I envy you Andrew, living in London with all that culture and those interesting artistic people. Me? It looks like I'll be stuck here in the sticks, rescuing sheep from barbed wire for the rest of my life."

Walter couldn't stop him, Andrew said. "Why don't you come and visit some day? I'll show you the sights."

Dafydd's face beamed. "Oh yes, that would be fantastic."

Walter hesitated, Andrew said: "Tell you what, I'll call around tomorrow or the next day and we'll swap addresses and things, OK?"

Dafydd nodded happily. "Da bo, see you." He sprang up the hill with the energy of a mountain goat.

Walter trudged slowly back through the outer gates of the adventure complex just in time for a late tea. As usual he sat alone and picked at the uninspiring food without relish. Betty came in, filled her plate, paying special attention to the mashed potatoes, and sat down opposite him. "You don't mind?" she asked as the first laden forkful found its way to her mouth.

Walter nodded.

"Well, how did your day go? Did you enjoy your solitary walk?"

"Yes thank you," said Walter. "Excuse me, I'm not very hungry, I think I'll go to my room."

Betty rolled her eyes, but let him go without protest and then got down to the really important business of cramming her mouth with the mash.

Alone in the austerity of the bedroom, Walter's mind filled the emptiness with torrents of thoughts and emotions. Walter or Andrew, who was he? Those people in the Welsh farmhouse had treated him like a real person, showed him respect. It had made him feel more alive, important, as if he had a purpose in life. He doodled on a writing pad over and over again, Andrew De Ville, he tried his signature, should it be *A Deville*? No that looked like something Satanic. What about *Andy*? too pally somehow. *Andrew De Ville* was fine, it suited him, his new personality. Why not? he thought, why shouldn't I be an interesting human being with a colourful background. He fell asleep early after the stresses of the first day of his new life.

Andrew intended to keep his promise and go back to the farm but the pressure of being Walter halted his feet and sent him around in circles in the grounds of the centre. The following day was no better; he spent most of the time in a trance watching daytime television in the lounge. In the afternoon he sat under a tree just outside the dormitory building and idly picked the heads off daisies and dandelions. The centre was approached from the main road by a drive with a wide tree-flanked entrance. He noticed a familiar figure hovering near the entrance and realised that it was the boy from the farm, Dafydd. Walter panicked, how could he keep up the pretence here so near to his real life? He prayed that Dafydd would keep his distance and pretended not to look in the direction of the entrance to avoid having to adopt the persona of Andrew.

Just then the two boys who had helped Walter into the reservoir came out of the main building. When they spotted Walter they began laughing and pointing like they'd done a few days earlier. They came close to him.

"Well hello, Wally, fancy a dip?" asked the smaller boy smiling maliciously.

The other doubled up with laughter. "No," he said, "he's enough of a drip already."

Walter would have dropped his head and waited for the crude tirade to pass but Andrew was on his feet, a fierce anger in his eyes that seemed to make him grow bigger, stronger, and more threatening. He felt invincible. Out of the corner of his eye he was aware of the now stationary figure, watching him from the bottom of the drive. That seemed to give him even more courage.

"You stupid worms," bellowed Andrew as he towered over them. "Now get out of here before I lose my temper."

The boys startled, looked questioningly at one another, then the larger one said: "Come on, let's go, he's not worth it, the girls will be waiting."

As the boys made their hasty exit with fake nonchalance, Andrew turned to face the entrance to the drive. Dafydd had gone. Andrew ran down to the road but there was no sign of him. Hold it, thought Walter, that's enough excitement before tea. Walter took all evening to recover. What was happening to him? This new world was exciting and frightening.

Friday, the last full day of the holiday, even Betty noticed how self-assured Walter had become.

"I think that you have benefited a great deal from this stay," she said, through mouthfuls of cornflakes.

Andrew smiled at her, she seemed so funny to him now, almost loveable, and the world was a different, brighter place. He was looking forward to this day. Today he would go back to the farm, confess all, and thank Dafydd and his mother for helping him come alive at last. He'd tell them of his hollow, empty life before their simple kindness and honesty set fire to his real self. After breakfast Andrew made his way happily to the reservoir and then to the farmhouse. The place was burned deep into his memory after the brief visit of the other day; the noises and smells of the farmyard greeted him like old friends. The day was bright and sunny, just right. Mrs Grufydd was scattering grain for the dozen or so noisy chickens that ran wild around the yard. He approached her from behind; her movements seemed slow, almost laboured.

"Bore da Mrs Grufydd," the new Welsh words came

out stilted with all the wrong sounds but at least he'd tried.

The woman seemed startled; she turned to face him. "Oh, it's you is it." Her face was drawn, her eyes red with tears.

"Are you all right?" Andrew didn't like seeing this strong capable woman in a moment of weakness.

"It's Dafydd," she said, "he's, he's gone . . ."

"Gone? Gone? What do you mean gone?"

"Come inside, I'll put the kettle on. I don't blame you really; it's his father you see."

Andrew followed meekly, what did she mean?

Mrs Grufydd took a few minutes to compose herself. She was silent as the tea brewed on the hotplate; after she poured it, she stared into the cup and spoke. "After you left that day, Dafydd couldn't stop talking about you; you and your posh life in London. I suppose it was bound to happen some day. He waited all the next day and the day after; even went to the centre to look for you, but he's shy you see, so I don't suppose he went in. When you didn't show up he became very sad, agitated. I've seen it all before, that look; he's got the wanderlust, just like his father before him. That man, he finally walked out on us nearly fifteen years ago, Dafydd can hardly remember him."

Walter was distraught, these were the only two people he'd ever cared for. What had he done with his stories and lies? Their lives had changed unalterably.

He said unconvincingly: "Don't worry, I'm sure he'll come back, do you know where he went?"

"Said he was going to London, to see the world, he

said, he'd write, he said . . ."

"It's OK, he'll be back, London's just like anywhere else, the streets are not paved with gold."

"Perhaps Andrew, perhaps he will, I don't know how I'll manage on my own."

"I'm sorry, it's my . . . "

"No, no, don't go saying that, you weren't to know, you can't help being what you are, but it all sounded so sophisticated to Dafydd, him stuck here out in the sticks as he called it."

If only she knew, thought Walter, Dafydd would soon discover the truth, he'd be back, Walter was certain.

Andrew had an idea. "Listen, the holiday finishes today but I've still got a few weeks left before I have to go back to school." This was untrue, as Walter had already decided to leave school, he had no intention of going back to do his A levels, not that he had the ability anyway. "If you like I can stay on and help around the place for a few days just until Dafydd comes back, Gran won't mind."

"I don't know, it's so soon."

Walter cringed at the commitment he was making but Andrew insisted. "Yes, I must, it will do me good to do some physical work for a change, you don't know how stifling it can be in the city. You wouldn't have to pay me, I'd do it for the experience and for food and a bed."

The days on the farm turned into weeks, Andrew kept the children's home happy by going to see Betty every week. She was glad to see him looking so healthy and happy and being of a lazy disposition never bothered to make the trek to the farmhouse to check it out. The boy was sixteen years old after all, as long as he could sustain himself he could be left to live his own life; anyway there were fresh batches of screwed up adolescents coming for her to practice her craft on. She counted Walter as one of her great successes and used his example often to prove her value in the Social Services department. Later in her career, his case notes helped her to climb the promotion ladder more than once.

Towards the end of the third week a letter arrived from Dafydd. Mrs Grufydd was overjoyed and she and Andrew celebrated with a market day visit to Carmarthen where she bought Andrew a new pair of denim jeans tailored to fit his leaner body. Dafydd reported that he was fit and well and had a job processing transparencies in a photographic studio off Baker Street. He was sorry but he'd decided to change his name to David Griffith because it had become too tedious to spell it out every time he met a new acquaintance. He promised to visit just as soon as he had the time, they were so busy at work and he'd met all sorts of interesting and famous photographers and models, they were really nice people, very down to earth.

The weeks turned into months, the months into years. Dafydd still hadn't revisited two years later but Mrs Grufydd made the long trip to London twice a year and came back to tell Andrew that Dafydd really was doing well. He'd been trained to take the actual photographs and he was good at it, building up quite a reputation for himself.

Andrew worked hard and enjoyed it; his years as a loner had prepared him well for the long days out in the fields or searching for lost sheep on the hills and in the woods.

It was early afternoon one summer day. Andrew broke through the undergrowth at the bottom of the hill near the reservoir and breathed deeply, a satisfied smile on his face. Walter was still there inside him but he was sort of sleeping contentedly, retired from active service at last. It had been raining heavily and the path around the Llyn was muddy and slippery.

A younger boy sat at the edge of the path; he looked downcast, withdrawn, he was wet and very muddy, just like one of Andrew's lost sheep. "Prynhawn da mate," said Andrew. "You all right?"

The boy grunted and turned away.

"Slipped in the mud have you?" Andrew said with a strong hint of a Welsh accent.

The boy mumbled shyly.

"From the Centre are you?"

The boy nodded.

"Come on then. Come with me, I don't bite. Mam will find you something to wear while you dry out. I might have some clothes in my wardrobe that will just about fit you."

Derek Wynford Jones

The Richest Man in the World

I am the richest man in the world. They say I am a recluse, I am afraid of doorknobs, I shower in purified water a dozen times a day, and I eat nothing but the flesh of sterilised fruit. It's true; I am the richest man in the world, the rest doesn't matter, it's of no consequence, it's irrelevant. All that matters is that these words reach you; that we touch.

I have no one you see – no mother, no father, no wife, no sons, no daughters, no family, no friends. Oh! I have slaves, paid slaves, unpaid sycophants, admirers, devotees even. I suspect that every second of every day my name is on the lips of someone; my name is typed into a search engine; my name is tweeted at the speed of light.

I live at a secret address in the city of London; from the outside, it merges into the streets, just another run-down multi-occupancy property. Inside, it's different – my private heaven, my private hell. I won't tell you where it is, you'll only tell the press, then I'll be besieged by hordes of desperate reporters with cameras and stupid questions. I'll be digested, twisted, corrupted, and regurgitated in little boxes, neatly wrapped and categorised, another item on the shelves of the super-psyche-market to be picked up, examined, eaten and defecated.

Aeons ago, in another life, I came from the swamps, just like you, fought for air until my lungs grew, shook the mud from my webbed feet and rolled in the sun on the damp grass. I lifted my eyes to the moon and the stars, and cried like a wolf. I fashioned a stick of wood

58

and dug out the sweet bodies of ants.

I shouted and screamed and laughed in the rain and danced on the graves of my enemies. I worshipped a God, I sucked a breast, I ran with the wind.

The streets of the city welcomed me, they bruised me and cut me, they fed me until they owned me. I learnt how to play their games, how to juggle their balls, how to hedge my bets, and eventually I won. I started to win and never stopped; now I have no need to play. The process is automatic, every day the treasures pour into my coffers like pins flying to a magnet, like water to the sea. I am the sea.

On the streets of the city, I am the dreamer, nothing will hurt me, it's under my control. I succumb to the dream. A bench in a park, I have nothing.

"Bit cold today mate! Bet you wish you'd worn a coat?"

"What? – cold, coat? Yes, you're right."

"Nice weather for the time of year though, innit?"

"Suppose so."

"'Ere, fancy a drink mate? Warm you up, a nice tot of whisky or something?"

"Sorry – got no money."

"That's OK mate, look, I've got a pocketful, it's a day off, got to take one sometimes, get away from the office, it's mad in there, like a bit of peace and quiet now and again, I do. You coming?"

"Two large whiskies – ta. Here, get that down you."

"Thanks."

What shall happen next, in my dream, how do I want it to develop? Stop – go with the flow.

"That's done the trick, want another? Go on, I'm buying."

"Thanks again."

"What's your name then? I'm Frank – Frank and honest, Ha! Ha!"

"I'm Rich, Richard."

"What do you do, Rich? Is that what they call you? Rich."

"Yes, that's what I'm called, I don't really do anything."

"On the dole eh? – Don't worry, I understand. Say, do you want a job? There's one going where I work. It's not much of a job, they need someone to look after the executive car park, you know, keep it clean, wash the cars, stop the plebs – like me – coming in. Ha! Ha! The last bloke done a runner, with the chairman's wife, would you believe?"

"Why not? That would be interesting."

In the basement, below the city, I sweep, I wash, I park the cars, the Jaguars, the large Mercedes, the unhappy chairman's Rolls-Royce. Frank runs the guts of the establishment; he is the porter, the caretaker, the cook, and the cleaner. I am his lower parts, the entrance to the womb of his empire. No questions asked, two hundred quid a week in my hand; it piles up in my unused shower cubicle, more unwanted cash to add to the pile. When will it end? This dream. I suspect that Frank has got me on the payroll, another John Smith – two hundred quid a week and the rest in his pocket – why not? I am a man without a life. How many others does he exploit in this way? His merchandise is lies, he uses me, he uses his masters and his garden of deceit flourishes.

I can see what is happening, Frank corrupts, a worm in the fruits of The Company, he turns the whole harvest rotten. In the dark corners of the car park he takes them aside, he has a quiet word. In exchange for packets of information, they give him bulging envelopes. Some of them cry and plead with him, he has no mercy. They are demoralised, robbed of their arrogance and the will to succeed.

Tea break – "Look Rich, it's the FT, the Financial Times, the nobs read this every day – idiots, they're idiots. See this article, it's about our Company, disastrous results. That lot couldn't organise a wedding – we're going down the pan. Ha! Ha!"

Twelve hundred quid later I decide I am tired; I am bored with the dream. I seek him out in a dark corner.

"Frank, I have a confession. I am Rich, really rich. I am the richest man in the world."

His reaction is immediate, intense, violent. "Get the hell out of here, stupid bastard, go away, don't come back; go back to your bench and your empty pockets."

I stand and stare, startled.

He pushes me hard. "Fuck off, d'you hear, fuck off!"

I am alone, on the street again, free again.

Back in my castle, I start to read the FT for the first time. I follow the fortunes of the Company – it continues, the fall of Frank's empire, their defeat is total; they are annihilated. Investigations are promised. What about the poor workers?

I pick up one or two of the reins of power, send for reports, analyses, stretch my fingers into remote parts of my empire. The global headquarters is inefficient, it has no coherent janitorial service. I instruct my executives, I am taking a personal interest. I want to vet the applicants for the job, we must have the right person.

Four weeks later the smells of the ripening fruit attract the right animal. It is him, Frank. Employ – I order, that's the one.

The worm is in, the decline can commence.

Now I withdraw again; wait for the fall, my liberation.

I am the richest man in the world.

I am the loneliest man in the world.

Chicken Caprice

"Hello!"

"Hello!"

"Is that …?"

"You're live on Radio Elchurch. How can I help you?"

"I, I, I …"

"You want to buy a chicken coop? Is that right Elwyn?

"Yes, I want to buy a small chicken coop for 5 or 6 hens."

"Only 5 or 6, how old are you Elwyn?"

"I'm going to be eleven years old, it's my birthday."

"Happy Birthday Elwyn, when is your birthday?"

"Next Sunday, I'll be eleven."

"So this chicken coop, is it a birthday present?"

"Yes, it's for my birthday."

"How many hens have you got?"

"None."

"No hens? Why do you want a chicken coop?"

"I'm getting some hens for my birthday."

"That's nice. Will you look after these hens properly?"

"Yes, but I need a coop first. A small one."

"Will you travel out of your area to get one if you need to? Where do you live Elwyn?"

"In Aberton, well – near Aberton."

"Will you be able to travel far to get a coop?"

"I'll ask – depends"

"Depends, OK. Will you look after the hens; will you feed them properly and look after them every morning and every night?"

"Yes."

"Why do you want to keep hens Elwyn? Do you want fresh eggs every day?"

"Yes."

"What sort of hens will you get Elwyn?"

"Don't know. Depends."

"Where will you get the hens?"

"Don't know, can I ask you to try and get some for me?"

"I'm sorry, we can't sell livestock on the Radio."

"Oh."

"But we can try and get you a chicken coop for five or six hens. Tell me Elwyn, what will you do with the hens when they get too old to lay eggs for you?"

"Uh? Don't know."

"Will you twist their necks until they snap? Or will you just cut off their heads with a sharp knife? Do you have a sharp enough knife Elwyn?"

"Uh?"

"Will you pluck their feathers yourself Elwyn? Will you cut open their bellies and pull out their intestines? Will you keep their livers and make chicken liver pate with them?"

"I don't know what you're talking about."

"Will you chop their bodies up to make soup? Will you tear off their legs and roast them on a spit?"

"Sorry?"

"Will you use their flesh to make chicken nuggets? Or will you make Chicken Caprice with them?"

"What's that?"

"Chicken Caprice. It's a wonderful dish. First you kill the chicken, then you cut the flesh off in big chunks, the bigger the better. Then you have to kill a pig. Yes that's right, a whole pig. Unless you know someone that's already killed a pig who has some of its flesh spare. You have to have a big slice of pig-flesh – bacon."

"But we don't keep pigs."

"Don't worry, you can buy some in the supermarket. Then you wrap the slice of pig-flesh around the chicken flesh and you cook it in butter."

"Butter?"

"Yes, butter. Now to get butter you're going to have to find a cow."

"That's all right, we do keep cows."

"Good, now get some milk from the cow. This is a very complicated process. You have to get permission from the government to take milk from cows, but it's all right, because they will give you money to help you, but you have to feed them and you have to inject them with chemicals and things, and you have to make them pregnant every year and then you have to take their babies away, because otherwise the baby cows will drink all the milk. We can't let that happen can we? Because we want the milk, why else would we keep the cows in the first place?"

"We've already got cows and we get plenty of milk from them, every day."

"Good, do you help with the milking Elwyn?

"Yes, sometimes, when I can."

"Good boy Elwyn. Your parents must be very proud of you. Now, you're going to need plenty of milk."

"Why?"

"Because you will need to make butter from it. And cheese, you need to make some cheese."

"Why?"

"Because after you've finished cooking the pig and the chicken in the butter you need to put cheese on it and cook it for a little bit longer."

"Mmm, sounds nice."

"Yes, it does doesn't it, but it gets a little more complicated. To make the cheese you need lots of cow's milk, but you also need something else."

"What's that?"

"Rennet, you need rennet."

"What's that?"

"That's easy, you know the baby cow that you took away from its mother so that you could have its milk?"

"Yes."

"Well – kill it. You have to kill it. It's no good to you anyway, because you'd have to feed it if you kept it

alive. You'd have to let it have the milk that you want
for yourself. You could sell it I suppose. There are
people who will buy the baby cows off you, but they'll
only kill it in the end anyway. So kill the baby cow."

"Why, what do I do with it then?"

"Well Elwyn, you have to cut it open. In its stomach it
has a special substance, that's the rennet I already
told you about. The baby cow uses the rennet to make
its mother's milk digestible. Here's the clever bit – you
can use the same rennet to help you to make cheese
from the cow's milk."

"Oh."

"So, now you've got the chicken flesh, the pig flesh,
the butter and the cheese and you can make Chicken
Caprice."

"Sounds lovely."

"It is Elwyn. Tell you what, leave your name and
address . . ."

"OK, it's Sunnyhill Farm . . ."

"No, don't tell me now. We don't allow callers to give
their addresses out on the air; you don't know what
kind of people are listening. I'm telling you Elwyn
there are some strange people out there. You wouldn't
believe the sort of things they get up to. Stay on the
phone and give your name and address to the
producer when I've finished talking to you."

"OK."

"Yes leave your address and I'll send you the recipe."

"I'd like that."

"Great, and if any other listener wants that recipe for Chicken Caprice I'll send it to them as well. Well thanks for calling Elwyn, it's been nice talking to you and good luck with the chicken coop."

"Thanks, bye"

"Oh Elwyn, before you go, what's your phone number? If someone has a chicken coop where should they phone?"

"It's 941678"

"Bye Elwyn"

"Right listeners, so if you have a spare chicken coop telephone Elwyn on 941678 and turn it into cash. Now who's on line 2 and what do you want to sell or buy?"

"Oh, hello – my name's Rebecca and I'm looking for a leather jacket!"

Tidying Up

He marched towards the anthill, spade held high above his head – he'd flatten it, get rid of those creepy-crawly invaders. How dare they set up camp on his lawn. It wasn't his fault it had been neglected. What was he supposed to do? He hadn't been allowed in the house, or the garden come to that for years. Never mind, she was gone now, never to nag or threaten him again. He was free to be himself. That's all he'd ever wanted after all.

He'd long suspected that she despised him; she resented the demands of their relationship and wanted to be on her own. She'd called him a vampire. What the hell was that supposed to mean? *A soul-sucking vampire*, the last thing she ever said to him, her very last words.

He threw the spade at the anthill. What did it matter now? There would be plenty of time to sort the garden out, plenty of time and plenty of money; at least she had left him that.

Angie was coming towards him across the unkempt grass. She had a can in each hand, cider for him in her right hand and lemonade for her in her left. That's how she did it, she always put him first. She handed him the cider. He kissed her on the cheek and put his arm around her, patting her pregnant stomach. She smiled and kissed him back.

"Welcome to your new home." He squeezed her shoulders. "Or should I say *selamat datang ke rumah baru anda.*"

She laughed. "You've been on that online translation site again haven't you."

"Shut up, I've been practising."

"I love you Graham," she said, kissing his cheek again. "Even though you have no idea how to speak Malay."

"Good thing your English is so good then, isn't it. You are perfect." He pulled her gently towards him and kissed her again.

A cat appeared from the overgrown shrubbery at the edge of the lawn. Angie leaned towards it and held out her hand. The cat rubbed itself against her, purring blissfully. Graham reached out to the cat as well – it pulled away from him and disappeared into the bushes.

He was disappointed and a little hurt but he remembered how lucky he was, living in his proper home again, and a beautiful lovely woman at his side. He wondered what the child would be like. He'd make sure it had everything and was treated well. He would dedicate the rest of his life to ensuring that it got the attention and respect it needed.

"What was it like? When you lived here with her? What was she like?" Angie asked.

In an instant all that warm goodness he'd felt inside himself turned into a scalding, searing maelstrom. He felt the anxiety and the anger scream inside his head. He squeezed Angie's arm – too tightly. She yanked herself away and retreated a few steps, looking at him nervously. He had to get away, get out, he had to do it now, before, before . . .

It took an hour of hard walking before he was

ready to go back, this was too important to jeopardise, he had to control himself, become master of the demons inside as well as the world outside.

Angie, as usual, didn't make an issue of his behaviour, she understood him instinctively, and always had, from the moment they had looked into each other's eyes. It was an immediate bond and he had never doubted it since, despite the circumstances of their first meeting.

Angie cooked an amazing curry – always did – never complained about having to cook, and he just knew that she put genuine love into that food. She didn't just rip open a few tins or massacre something in the microwave. He'd never eaten so well in his life and he knew it was doing him good.

"I don't know how you do it Angie," he said. "Gold star every time."

She blushed. "You're worth it Graham – never forget it. Besides, it's not me, it's nature, she is providing the raw materials – the fruits, the vegetables, the herbs and the spices, that's the secret."

"I wish I'd known all that before," he said. "Then maybe things wouldn't have got to where they have." He felt the regret rising inside him again. If only he'd taken action sooner, if only he'd known Angie then. Then it wouldn't have ended in such a mess. He sighed.

Angie reached across the table and took his hand in hers. "It's OK now Graham. Everything will be OK."

And he knew she was right, after all he wouldn't have met her if things had been different. "You're a bloody marvel Angie – that's what you are, if only . . ."

"Ssh Graham. What's the point of all that. This is where we are. This is what we have to deal with."

And so it went for the first three months. Every day he felt stronger, every day he healed a little more. He learned to deal with the scars, with the after-effects. And then the baby was born, a fantastically robust boy, a boy who would need all the love Graham could muster, a boy he was determined would get every advantage possible. Angie would be a good mother. Angie would make up for everything.

Graham managed to sit up in bed and hold the baby, his beautiful boy Alfie, just 6 months old and already bursting with character. Later, in a pause between her motherly duties, Angie came into the room and sat at Graham's bedside.

"Are you comfortable?" she asked.

Graham smiled and nodded. "Yes darling, and do you know what? I think I'm ready to forgive her. It's all thanks to you, my Angie, my angel."

"Oh stop it Graham. I've told you before."

"Perhaps it's seeing you with Alfie. She wasn't always a bad mother. In a way, I'm glad she never got to know about the cancer. I can't imagine anything worse, knowing that your child is going to die before you."

"Well, you didn't die."

"I know, but I am dying now. I know it, and do you know what. It's all right, it's OK, it really is now. I've had my remission. More than that, I finally got a life."

"Ssh Graham, you don't really know."

"Yes Angie, I do know, and you do. After all – that's how we met. You know more about what's going on inside me than I do."

"I love you Graham. Never forget that. Promise me."

"I know Angie, and you promise me that you will go back to work as we agreed when Alfie is a year old. The world needs people like you Angie, you've made my life worth something and you can do it for others, and I'm not talking about our personal relationship – that's a beautiful bonus, but you are a brilliant doctor, a true healer."

Graham suddenly weakened. "I'm tired," he said.

He sank into the bed smiling up at Angie. He'd done it. Everything was in place; he couldn't do another thing that would make a difference. Ah, he'd had a good life.

Jimmy Jones 2014

Jimmy Jones didn't need much; just a good meal once a day and a shag now and again. The meal he could sort out for himself; for the shag, of course, he needed someone else. The women he chose were generally reasonably attractive, independent, and up for it, no commitments, no expectations, that sort of thing.

He worked in a small studio in Cathays, Cardiff. The studio was nothing more than his landlady's garage with a long extension lead hooked up to a kitchen power point for electricity. She let him have it as part of the reasonable rent he paid for the sparse studio flat he'd lived in since he split up with his wife six years earlier, when he was 37.

Since then, he'd made a good job of re-inventing himself. After the bankruptcy and the divorce he'd needed to; there was no way he was going to expend another precious breath on that shit, the shit that 'ordinary people', whatever they are, call normal: ambition, holidays, mortgages, that sort of thing. All that nonsense about work/life balance; it wasn't so much balancing but running from one end of the slide to the other ad infinitum and getting too tired, and having to concentrate so much on staying 'balanced' that you didn't have time to just be whatever you are. That world baffled Jimmy; he couldn't cope with it at all. It just didn't suit him; so, Jimmy Jones was now an artist.

He turned from the computer screen as Cristal pushed open the door of the studio and found himself smiling; he hadn't expected her but she would definitely brighten up a dull afternoon.

"I'm not stopping," she said.

"Oh." His smile flattened.

"Just thought I'd pop in and see how you are. After the exhibition and all that."

"Fine," he said. "I'm OK, sold a few"

"How many?"

"Enough." Jimmy didn't need much and what he did need he could provide for with the sale of his paintings. He didn't really sell many and when he did he didn't get a lot for them, not a lot – but enough.

"Anyway," Cristal said, "I'm popping to the Co-op, just wondered if you wanted anything."

Jimmy mentally checked his inventory of essentials. He didn't really want anything, but he wanted an excuse for Cristal to come back, maybe he could talk her into staying for a bit.

"I could do with some sugar, and I'm a bit low on tobacco."

"OK, half an ounce enough?"

"Yeah, and a packet of those green skins."

His gaze moved appreciatively up and down her body as he spoke; his eyes met hers. She smiled. He'd never been able to work her out properly; maybe that's why they were still shagging after nearly a year.

He remembered the day they met in the Co-op in Crwys Road. He was in the queue for the checkout and she was in front of him. It was her hair that first caught his attention, blonde and straight and shoulder-length, obviously from a bottle but done tastefully. He edged a little closer to try and get a look at her face to see if it matched up to the allure of the hair. When she turned to her left to look at the wine he wasn't too disappointed; she was pretty all right, in a common sort of way; not thin, but not enough bulk to complain about, in fact her round, full face, lightly tanned with feint freckles complemented her hair nicely.

He edged a little closer again to see if he could get a better look at her cleavage, which he'd glimpsed briefly when his eyes fell from her face. Here was another pleasant surprise. She had a white T-shirt on under a black jacket, open at the front. Her breasts were obviously big but not flabby. The T-shirt was fairly low cut so that he could see the same pleasantly tanned skin that was on her face, covering the top of her breasts but with just half an inch of cleavage showing. He liked that. Lower down she wore faded blue jeans that clung without straining and showed off her lower curves without strangling her waist. He liked that too. But it was the red shoes that did it. He was hooked.

She turned again and reached her hand out to pick up a bottle of wine, Argentine Malbec, a cheap but decent red. Her arm touched his chest as she leaned over and he felt an unexpected jolt that made him start.

"Oh, sorry," she said with that smile that he would come to associate with a warm sexual satisfaction.

Cristal turned out to be the perfect shag; not just the bodily bit, which was very satisfying in itself, but also the gift she gave of an uncomplicated relationship. He didn't know much about her apart from the obvious physical stuff; it didn't bother him and it didn't seem to bother her either. He knew she was financially comfortable because of the mid-range designer clothes she wore and the expensive perfume. She was a feast for the senses and a pleasure on the brain because she didn't make any demands.

While Cristal was in the Co-op, Jimmy washed under his arms and put a clean T-Shirt on, the newish grey one with that covered his belly and showed off his masculine shoulders. It was freshly washed and smelt a bit too strongly of the cheap washing powder from the launderette, but it was covered in blotches and streaks of bright acrylic paint, a look he knew turned her on.

When she came back she laughed.

"What's funny?" he asked.

"Oh, it's nothing. Here's your sugar and tobacco."

"Ta," he said, taking them off her and putting them on the desk in front of the computer monitor.

"Right then," she said, "I'd better be off. Things to do and all that."

"Can't you stay for a cup of tea or something?"

Cristal looked at her watch, a petite white gold affair, something else that complemented her hair and her skin colour.

"All right then. I'll make it. What do you want?"

"A cup of Chai would be nice."

Jimmy watched as Cristal made the Chai in the makeshift tea-making station he'd created from old cardboard boxes and a broken chair. The Chai was something else aromatic she'd introduced him to; it seemed to go with her, like the hair and the watch and the jeans, and of course the red shoes. He hoped she'd stay; he was getting aroused.

"Why have you never asked me to pose for you?" she said, as she sat on the bedraggled couch next to the computer desk.

He looked down at her from the cheap swivel chair he was sitting in. This wasn't like Cristal; asking questions that needed thinking about. He was surprised. He sipped the sweet hot Chai but didn't respond other than with a slight lift of his eyebrows; he needed time to figure this one out.

"Well?" she asked. "Am I not attractive enough or something?"

"That's not fair, I hardly ever paint from life."

"But you've got pictures of women everywhere."

"They're mostly from my head," he said. He felt himself getting defensive. He didn't need to justify himself to Cristal; they didn't have that kind of relationship.

"I used to be a mess," she said.

"Oh." Why was she telling him this now?

"When I was younger. Especially after I had my first child."

"First child?"

"Yeah, two, they're nine and seven years old."

Jimmy shifted in his chair, one eye on the unfinished game of Gem Catcher on the computer screen. Now he wanted her to go, but he felt he had to say something; he owed her some respect after 11 months of shagging.

"You'd never know, you've got a lovely bo . . . I mean you've never mentioned them before."

"No," she said. "They're not with me anymore."

"With their father?" Jimmy asked.

"My mother, in Bristol."

"Oh."

"Have you got any kids?"

Now he was cornered. Of course he had kids, three of them, but he hardly ever saw them. They were comfortably ensconced with his ex-wife and her new husband in a tidy suburb of Swansea.

"Yeah, sort of."

"Have you got any photos of them?"

"Somewhere."

"Did you ever paint them, or their mother?"

"Not really. Do you really want me to paint you?"

"I was just wondering, that's all."

"Let's go for it then."

"Now?"

Cristal gave him a look that scoured his expression for signs of sincerity. He smiled as benignly as he could.

"OK then," she said. "How do you want me?"

Jimmy didn't know how to answer that one; the truth was that he had never painted a live model in his life. Did he want her sitting demurely on the edge of the couch? Did he want her spread-eagled naked on the floor? Did he want her arranged into an elaborate and uncomfortable artistic pose? Then he realised, what he wanted more than anything was for her to be quiet and stop telling him things about herself and asking questions about himself. He came to a decision.

"I want you to stand up next to that shelf over there, facing away from me and my easel. I want you to turn slightly to the left and hold your arm out as if you're just about to take a bottle of red wine from a shelf in a supermarket."

She laughed.

"But you'll have to be quiet; I need to concentrate on the visuals, on the composition, on the light. Conversation will distract me. It's critical to get the initial outline of the painting done. It's crucial to concentrate. That's when the art is born, at that moment when you first put your brush to the canvas."

"OK."

She obeyed his instructions and he moved over to the easel that had a blank canvas positioned on it ready to go. He'd been waiting for inspiration while playing Gem Catcher, something he'd been doing so much of lately that he could feel the early stages of carpal tunnel syndrome creeping up again. At least painting, for him, wasn't done in a series of repetitive movements, and he always tried to use both hands to achieve balance.

He retrieved a number 16 brush from the jar of dirty water where he'd shoved it the day before the exhibition, after hastily adding his signature, *Jimmy Jones 2014*, to the last three in a series of seventeen specially created abstract works. It was those 40 inch abstracts that kept him in sugar and tobacco and away from the world of 9 to 5 that he despised and feared so much. Most of his clients were young professionals who wanted a piece of original art to hang on the sterile off-white walls of their new or refurbished houses and apartments that infested Cardiff Bay, Pontcanna and the posher parts of Roath. He was proud of his abstracts; he felt that they added some light and peace to the frenzied bleak lives the poor buggers had to live in order to feel valued in the crazy Maya that was post-industrial Britain.

Jimmy squeezed a dollop of cadmium red the size of a squashed tomato onto a paint-encrusted saucer that he'd borrowed from his landlady's kitchen Then he wiped the brush dry in a linen tea towel, stiff with old paint, and pushed it deep into the slowly spreading mound of red.

"Do you want me to take my coat off?" Cristal asked.

Jimmy lifted his hand towards the canvas.

"No," he said.

He drew the outline quickly, and stood back to see if the composition made sense. Then he had an idea. He would put a mirror in front of Cristal and paint that along with her reflection. That meant he'd get to see the allure of her hair from behind and the beauty of her face and breasts from the front at the same time.

He sketched the mirror and the reflection. The cadmium red on the saucer lasted just long enough.

"Right," he said.

"What, have you finished already?"

Jimmy laughed. "No. Stay there."

"I'm moving away, leaving Cardiff," she said.

"Oh." Non-committed caution was always his first reaction; he liked to have time to think before deciding what his second should be.

"Yeah, it's my sister, in London. Her housemate moved out. She's been on at me for years."

Jimmy reached for a large tube of Mars Black and without thinking squeezed it directly onto the canvas in a zigzag motion.

"It was her that helped me after the kids; helped me to sort myself out. I lost it for a bit. That's why the children are in Bristol with my mother. I see them every weekend though."

That explained it, Jimmy thought. He'd assumed that she had a husband somewhere, who was probably in work every weekday.

"I'm hoping to have them permanently soon, but they're happy enough."

"Oh." Jimmy mixed some of the black into the edges of the red creating a deep purple. It needed white, lots of white.

"What about your kids?" she asked.

Jimmy cleared his throat. "Um. When are you going?"

"Don't know when exactly, soon I suppose."

Jimmy felt the old familiar sadness and loneliness return. He didn't like to think too much about his children. He missed them so much; they were happy though, happier than they'd been for years. It had taken a long time after the divorce for them to readjust. He couldn't help it, the sadness became too strong, it overwhelmed him. He started to cry silently.

"Are you all right," she asked.

Jimmy cleared his throat again. "Yes," he said. "Please don't say anything for a minute, I'm concentrating."

Cristal looked over her shoulder and nodded. Jimmy managed a weak smile. She turned back into her position.

Jimmy reached out for the Titanium White, but his hand picked up the Cobalt Blue instead. He squeezed half the tube onto the edges of the canvas, thinking perhaps it could be the background colour, reminiscent of a clear blue sky, but it looked too dark. He lightened the bottom corners with a few squirts of Process Yellow creating a streaky melange of greens and blues.

"It's still too dark." He didn't realise he'd said it aloud until Cristal responded.

"What's too dark?" she asked, turning to face him.

He looked down to avoid her gaze and noticed that she had the red shoes on. Somehow that sparked the sadness off again and he couldn't help himself; he started crying properly, his body heaving uncontrollably.

"What's the matter?" she asked, moving towards him.

"I'm sorry, sorry."

She put her arms around him and pulled him close. He felt the warmth of her body through their clothes and the softness of her face against his. He started to regain his composure as she hugged him.

"It's all right," she said. "It's OK."

He rubbed his face against hers, then kissed her softly on the cheek. He couldn't face the thought of not having her there with him. "Don't go."

She disengaged herself from him and took a step

back. She looked puzzled. "What?"

"Don't go. I love you."

She laughed.

Jimmy wanted to erase the last few moments and those dangerous words, or else cover them up with a thick coat of acrylic like he could when he fucked up a painting, but of course he couldn't; and he realised, he did actually love her.

"I'm sorry," he said.

"But I love you too. Didn't you know? I thought . . . I thought you didn't care."

He cried again, but in a different way; her eyes were damp as well. They embraced. It came to him then why everything about Cristal seemed so right, how everything went together. Now he was part of that too, part of her life, part of her being. He needed her more than anything.

"What now?" he asked.

"What about the painting?" she asked. "Is it finished?"

"Just about, it needs some white though, lots of white. Hang on."

Jimmy pulled himself away from her long enough to fill in every gap in the painting with a thick coat of Titanium White and sign his name on the bottom right of the canvas – *Jimmy Jones 2014.*

Us

I walk slowly, tussling with possibilities - another big change looming. I shouldn't have to face such uncertainty now, my sixtieth birthday tomorrow and here I am, not knowing where I will sleep next week or what I will do to pay the bills. I remember taking a drunken oath on my twentieth birthday that I would retire before forty. Surely twenty years is long enough to find my place in this world and to make a million or two - I thought. I left home that year and did not return for a decade, lots of reasons, none of them mattered now.

A wisp of cold air brings goosebumps to my bare arms. Perhaps I should go back to the car for my jacket? I look around, nearly there, I'll be OK. The sign stills hangs above the shop, rocking now in the cold wind. I notice the absence of traffic in the street; there are no people either, no sound except the growling air. There is an unfamiliar arrangement of clouds, hundreds of greying candy-floss pillows huddled, the bright blue beyond leaking round their edges.

I push the shop door; the same metallic ring of the bell announces my presence. There is no one in the shop. I expect the person who runs it now to emerge smiling, stifling a yawn. I wonder who it will be this time. Ten years ago it was an ageing German man, still eager, but very tired; ten years before that a friendly Irish woman. The first time I came back, the day before my thirtieth birthday, they were still here of course. That was hard for me, harder for them I suppose. They had changed in that decade, and I had, at first, regretted staying away for so long. So many regrets, so many failures, so many wrong turns – how can I possibly choose the right direction now? I don't suppose it matters, it will be wrong whatever I decide. Maybe I never really had any choice, and don't have a choice now. Maybe I will do the only thing possible – whatever that is; it will be done and that's that. Maybe choice is an illusion, we are products of the universal energy that began in nothing and will end in nothing, pellets of consciousness whizzing through time to its end.

I am browsing the bookshelves. This corner, it seems, is dedicated to pristine copies of mid-twentieth century literature. There is Nineteen Eighty-Four, in its original paperback edition, an array of Neville Shutes and an imported first edition of Atwood's The Handmaid's tale.

The bell rings behind me. I turn my head enough to recognise the shape of a middle-aged man. I hear him sigh and trundle to another corner of the shop.

A few days with them over my thirtieth birthday shredded the already fragile fabric of my maturity and composure and I was gone again for a decade. I returned on the eve of my fortieth. It was too late of course, both had gone. The Irish woman told me they had died within a month of each other, nearly ten years earlier. She couldn't remember who went first. I didn't tell her who I was.

I'm thumbing the pages of The Hobbit. It was the only book I'd taken with me that first time, something to do with the journey. I still have it, I think, lost in the mound of detritus gathered since. I never finished it then and still have not. This book is the same edition, in mint condition, like the others on these shelves.

The door dings again and slams hard so that I instinctively turn. In my peripheral vision, the middle-aged man also looks towards the door. It is dark in the shop and the light from outside silhouettes the nervous figure of another man, fidgeting and shuffling his feet. We both look back to our books, maybe he'll go away. I do not want to talk to him.

It's like this in the gents' in the museum, men facing walls, not acknowledging each others' presence, force-fields of mutual suspicion and embarrassment creating bubbles of protection. Protection from what? I think. Maybe it's time to open up to this mad, bad world, maybe if I do then the choices I make will be easier, obvious. Maybe they will be right at last.

Another minute passes and there is still no shopkeeper; just us, three strangers in a quiet bookshop on a deserted street on a darkening late autumn evening. I look across at the same counter I'd worked at that last summer. Why should things change when there is no need for change? I remember that from my last visit, by then it was obvious, it had become a pilgrimage, some sort of compulsion that came over me once a decade – a journey to my Sargasso Sea for a rebirth. The German man lived according to his very personal ethics, a mismatch of environmental awareness and meanness. At least he had his values and his purpose. I had spent an hour listening to his earnest advice, but he was wrong, things do change – change is life.

Once again the bell sings; the door swings open and is closed carefully. A young man appears in the shadows, and hesitates before moving softly towards the counter. Outside there is a strong blast of wind and the sign shudders against its frame. It's getting darker.

I'm getting impatient now; perhaps it's time to go? I have made the journey back; my duty to myself is done. There are no answers here, and after sixty what does it matter anyway? I am me now, fossilising slowly into my old age. I will never be anyone else. Maybe that's it? The liberation from ambition, the end of dreaming, hoping for change. It's just breath after breath until I die, a life lived after all.

The light outside dims again. The lights inside flicker as the wind hurls its force against the building. I look around to observe the reactions of the others in the shop and notice another young man, barely more than a boy, behind the counter. The other three are staring at him.

The boy-man taps the counter. "Right," he says. "You are all here."

A sudden nauseous panic explodes in my stomach and surges to every cell in my body. There is a terrible feeling of complete recognition. I reach for a shelf to steady myself. Now I have to search out the faces of the other men. Anchoring myself to the bookshelf, I look around, scanning their features in the dim light, they are all doing the same. Each of us has the same expression of bewildered terror.

The man-boy at the counter says in a clear, commanding voice: "Don't panic, this is my doing."

We all turn to look at him.

He is the youngest.

"Yes," he says, "you are all my future selves and I am your past self." He turns to me. "You are, I suppose, the oldest. Sixty tomorrow? Is that right?"

I respond with a nod that becomes repetitive.

"And you," he says, turning to the middle-aged self, "are fifty." Then he points at the other two, "forty — thirty — and I am twenty tomorrow."

Thirty-self is the first to react intelligibly. "Wow, man!"

Yes, he is, I was, still capable of cosmic surprise at that age.

Forty-self slaps himself on the side of his head. When I was, I am — his age I still bristled with vigour. I wasn't able to decide if I was young or if I was old, but I knew I was still fighting, still strong. Forty-self is agitated, his head turning from one to another of us in wide eyed jerks.

Mr Fifty is fat and moves his head lethargically with a faded nod. He was before the synthetic hormones used to boost my lazy thyroid kicked in — I feel for him. It was pretty tough for me at fifty. I had come to the shop as usual, despite the turmoil in my life. When I returned home she was different, quieter; a few weeks later she moved out.

He looks me up and down and sighs. "I see I survived then," he says with a tired smile.

I cannot help but smile back; how quickly I am adapting to this new reality.

The nausea has passed leaving a warm numbness throughout my body.

The Twenty-self commands: "Listen."

We all give him our attention.

"OK," he says to himself with a deep breath. "I know this is not real but I can cope, I can handle it. Just remember, remember to breathe."

He takes another deep breath and addresses the four of us. "I know – OK – I know you are not real – you are phantasms, manifestations of possible future selves. You are not real but you are here, here for a reason."

"Wait up," says Forty-self. "What do you mean I am not real? How can I not be real? I know who I am. I know I am. I am."

Thirty-self laughs nervously. "This is too much," he says. "I am in the shop, I'm nearly thirty years old. I can see. I can hear. I am here."

I cannot reach those two – they are lost. I am a different person now. I wait my turn.

"Yes," Fifty-self sighs, "this is it. This must be it. Nothing makes sense. I am dying, I must be dying. Why should anything make sense if I am dying?"

"OK," I say. "I'll go along with this for a bit. Maybe when I wake up I will have learned something. I don't think I'm dying. This doesn't feel like dying. Dying is nothing, this feels like something."

"Right," says the youngest self. "You are not dying or dreaming, you are not mad, you are not anything, you are just not. Well, not in the material sense at least, but I suppose you are – in whatever state of being this is. Anyway, no time for this, we've got things to do, things to talk about – before you fade."

Now here is someone I can empathise with. Poor sod hasn't yet felt the pain. I'm still willing to play along, to be the passive observer. I'm nearly sixty anyway, accelerating towards oblivion, this has to be better than oblivion. At least I'm alive. I am still aware of myself. There is no doubt – this is my reality.

"Thing is," Twenty-self says, "I need help. It's a crucial decision, it could, it will, affect the rest of my – our – life. OK, I know it's not a big deal, human beings make choices every day that lead to massive change."

"Chaos theory," offers Forty.

"The millennium bug," Fifty-self laughs.

"It's not me that's mad," says Thirty.

I'll top that I think, and blurt out: "The Higgs boson particle, Facebook, Twitter, online shopping."

"Listen," the boy-man commands again. "You've got to let me speak – hang on – that's up to me. Must breathe. Remember to breathe."

He closes his eyes and breathes in, slowly, deeply. He exhales and opens his eyes.

"It's simple really. Should I stay or should I go? No, don't answer that. I don't need to know that – yet. In theory you should all know the answer to that, since you are my future selves, versions of them at least."

Forty-self begins shaking his head vigorously. He jumps up and down and punches a row of books.

"That hurt," he says. "I'm real."

Thirty-self shakes his head. "Shut up, it's me, I'm the real one – look."

He twists his head to reveal the side of his neck – a

large bruise and a barely healed cut.

"That's where the rope caught me on the boat last week – it still hurts."

"I get a boat?" says Twenty.

I feel for the scar on my neck, the others do the same. It is still there, lost among the creases.

"This is daft," I say. "Of course I am the real one. I am the oldest. If this had happened, I'd remember it. I'd have remembered it at twenty, remembered it at thirty, forty and fifty, and I'd remember it now."

I chuckle. Why am I getting drawn into this? This must be a prank. But it feels real all right, as much as anything else I've experienced has felt real – clever though. Who would go to so much trouble to play such an elaborate trick on me?

My Fifty-self shakes his head and sighs.

"What's next?" He sighs again and looks at his feet. "Om mani padme hum," he starts to chant. We all stand transfixed as these ancient words resonate with some inner tuning fork, creating a vibration that possesses my attention so that I don't remember where I am. I don't even think to ask the questions. For a few moments I just am.

The Maya returns with a hysterical laugh from Mr Forty. Ah, I think, that's where I am, I remember now. Breathe. Remember to breathe. This is my reality and I have to deal with it.

Twenty-boy slaps his hand on the counter. "Maybe they are right, maybe it is wrong to fiddle with your brain like this. Maybe it's best to stick to best bitter and a whisky at Christmas. Stay off the acid – too late now – too late now."

"Hang on," says Forty-me. "I get it. This is a flashback, of course, it happens every time."

"Yes," says Fifty-man. "I remember. It does."

"But we must forget in between," says Thirty-self. "Is that right?"

"But which one is real?" asks Twenty-self. "Yes, that's it. That's what this is all about."

"How about we don't forget it this time – we make sure we remember. How do you think we can do that? There must be a way," says Thirty.

They all turn and stare at me. I stare back, focussing on my breathing.

"You are the oldest. You must know," they all chant in unison.

I do remember now, and I remember this as well – it's hopeless, it will continue until I die.

"So, where is Seventy-self?" asks Forty.

"And Eighty?" adds Thirty.

Even Ninety, I think. Why not Ninety? That's it then for me, this is the last time. I will be free of this. I don't want to remember. This will pass and I will forget again.

Suddenly Thirty-me walks quickly towards the door. He opens it. Through the doorway the outside has become dark; the wind lobs sprays of rain into the shop. He pauses and looks back at us. His expression is blank. He turns and walks into the night. The door slams after him.

"Shit!" says Twenty-me. "One down. I need answers quick."

Forty-self starts to hyperventilate. "Sorry," he says. "I'm not handling this very well; I'm not ready for this."

As he leaves he chants to himself: "This too must pass . . . this too must pass . . ."

Fifty-man sighs loudly, a long low groan. He stares at the floor and walks steadily towards the door.

There's just the two of us now.

I turn to the other me: "What now?" I ask. "I feel no inclination to go."

He shrugs. "It's nearly over."

I walk over to the counter and look deep into his eyes.

That's weird. I'm sure there was someone here. Never mind, I've had enough of this creepy place and those two upstairs. There's a great big world out there, beyond that door. I'll tolerate my twentieth birthday tomorrow and then leave. It might be hard and I'll probably get hungry from time to time, and cold in the coming winter, but it will be worth it. I've got my whole life ahead; I wonder what will become of me?

The Last Fare

He discovered it early on Friday evening and put it quickly in his pocket – too astonished to accept the reality of what it could mean. He needed time to think it through; perhaps it wasn't what it seemed; perhaps it didn't matter. Anyway, he had to get to work; his first fare of the night was waiting, no doubt reeking of cheap aftershave and already smelling of alcohol.

She was still in the bath.

He put his hand over the white glossed balustrade, flicked a fleck of loose paint off with his index finger and turned his mouth up towards the bathroom, "I'm off," he raised his voice only a little, not bothered whether she heard him or not. "I've got a pick up, see you later."

He didn't expect acknowledgement and he didn't get any. He slammed the white uPVC door behind him, crossed the pavement of the narrow, car-choked street and got into the taxi.

The green Jaguar XJ6 was ageing gracefully, almost a classic now. He knew he should have already replaced it to maintain his credibility as a cab driver but he couldn't. His excuse was that it would cost too much, but that was bollocks. It already cost him too much in breakdowns and subsequent lost fares but he couldn't replace it just yet; this wasn't the time to be getting entangled in a four or five year finance deal, it wasn't possible. In fact there wasn't much that was possible, he felt like he was stuck in a holding pattern, just waiting for the all clear to get on with his life.

The XJ6 had once been his company car. When he lost his job they let him keep it as part of the redundancy pay-off, but that was ten years ago when it was already past its best. There he was then, coming up to 40, twenty grand and a car; what could he do?

After six months of fruitless job seeking his twenty grand had halved and she was giving him so much hassle that he reluctantly took the suggestion from his old mate Dewi and joined him as a taxi-driver in a loose partnership.

Now he was getting hassle again, the partnership had become so loose it had fallen apart, although they were still good friends. His residual income was meagre. She was earning more than he was in her job as assistant manager of a shoe shop in the new shopping centre and still banging on about money; berating him because Dewi had acquired a fleet of clean modern cars and lived in a new town house on the waterfront, while they were still stuck in the pokey terrace on the edge of town.

Then there was that discovery – the damn phone.

He drove the Jaguar lazily through the too-familiar terraced streets; he could have done it with his eyes closed if it wasn't for the other cars and the pedestrians, who insisted on driving and walking randomly respectively. He teased the car around Asda, effortlessly dodging the dregs of the evening's shoppers as they emerged nervously from the car park in their characterless fuel efficient carriages laden with the comestibles and consumables they needed to ensure survival for the next seven days, and drifted down Murray Street towards the traffic lights at the Station Road junction. The usual pratts were gathering outside the pubs and bars volunteering their bodies for medical research into the effects of massive overdoses of alcohol and other so-called recreational drugs.

He turned left at the green light and cruised on along the road. He negotiated the level crossing and the top end of New Dock Road, then turned left towards the Morfa and zipped past more cramped terraces before parking outside the address in Ropewalk Road. He switched the engine off, yawned and lit a cigarette, glad of the few wasted moments to mull over the consequences of what he had found. He lifted the cigarette towards his mouth and with his other hand explored the smooth cool body of the mobile phone in his pocket.

It was a new model, silver and sleek, better than the chunky pay-as-you-go lump of blue plastic that his diminishing business depended on; no doubt it had a built in HD camera as well. He removed his hand from his pocket – it would keep.

The blue plastic lump on the dashboard shuddered and uttered a weak facsimile of *The Simpson's* theme tune. He picked it up and stared at the screen – it was her. He answered it anyway.

"Hello."

"Just wondering when you think you'll be back."

"Why?"

"Just wondering, Julie's asked me to pop over."

"It's Friday, I'll be busy. You know that."

"Sorry, just checking."

"Bye."

Just checking what? He had a fair idea. Maybe the phone in his pocket would give him the confirmation. There was no doubt that she had little respect left for him, and he was almost certain that she had stopped loving him as well. He could cope with that, for a while anyway, but as time went on he found himself losing his love for her, and that he couldn't cope with.

The man came out of the terraced house; he was tall and thin, wearing a short-sleeved check shirt and a pound of grease on his just-cropped dark hair, in his late twenties probably. An older woman followed him out of the house and pressed what looked like a couple of twenties into his hand. The guy looked at Colin and raised his eyebrows as he deftly pocketed the notes. He raised his eyebrows again before giving what Colin assumed was his mother a quick peck, and yanking open the back door of the Jaguar.

Arrogant twat.

Colin did a quick three-point turn and drove back towards the town centre.

"Mothers aye," the young man said, looking at Colin via the rear-view mirror.

"Aye," Colin said, making it clear from his tone that he wanted a quiet ride.

And they did, cruising through the station gates and along Station Road where the pavements were already overflowing with midriff-challenged young women and young men of the same ilk as the passenger.

"The Diplomat is it?" Colin asked as they passed

the old Town Hall, its high metal gates sealed for the night against attacks from pissed teenagers.

"Nah, it's the Thomas Arms."

"I was told The Diplomat when the booking was made."

"Mothers!" The passenger probably raised his eyebrows again but Colin wasn't looking.

A man's figure appeared from nowhere and fell against the front of the car. Luckily Colin was driving slowly; he braked hard and instinctively leapt out of the car. The bloke he'd nearly run over was leaning on the green bonnet and puking too close to the headlights.

"What the fuck," Colin said, tugging the sleeve of the man's shirt.

He noticed the blood then and the two shadows running through the trees of the Sunken Gardens and towards the Sheesh Mahal Indian restaurant in Stepney Street.

"Did they do this?"

"Fuck off – it's fuck all."

The man jerked himself away from Colin and staggered off in the same direction that the two men had run in.

Colin shrugged and turned back to his car. Fuck it, he thought.

His passenger had gone, he could see him trotting past the Corner House shop and ducking into Vauxhall where he could take a short cut through West End and up Goring Road to the Thomas Arms. Colin started the car and accelerated after him. By the time he turned into Vauxhall the passenger was past the health club and making good ground towards the pedestrian access to West End.

Colin accelerated again. The bloke looked back over his shoulders and ran faster. A car came out of the lane behind the council offices and Colin had to slow down to avoid a collision. The passenger disappeared around the corner onto the main road.

Never mind, Colin thought, I know where he's going and I know where he lives. He turned the XJ6 around in the empty car park at the end of Vauxhall and drove slowly towards the exit to the main drag, intending to drive to the Thomas Arms and confront the little shit. He'd had so much trouble over his years as a taxi driver that nothing surprised him anymore; he remembered the time when he'd dropped a twenty quid fare outside a posh semi in Burry Port and the stupid fucker had run in and slammed the door without paying. Colin had called the police that time.

The car stalled opposite the chemist, just short of the old British Legion.

"Bollocks," he said to himself. What a job. What a town; he was fed up with them both, sometimes it was just too much for him and all the time there she was nagging and prodding. That was the only good thing about his job; he could always say he was working and leave her alone with her catalogues and brochures whenever she got too much for him.

He couldn't start the car; the usual bonnet opening and WD40 trick didn't work; now he'd have to phone Dewi and humiliate himself again. Dewi would sort it out; he always sorted everything out. He'd send one of his drivers along, one who was a passably-good mechanic as well, probably Tone the Drone, god he was boring, but then it would be better than being stranded in town with a dud car on a Friday night.

Dewi didn't answer his mobile, so Colin phoned his office; he was out on a job they said, but they'd send a man anyway. While Colin waited he finally pulled the silver mobile from his pocket and turned it over in his hand. It felt good, still cool and nicely heavy for its size. It glistened with orange light from the streetlamps. It was switched off. He pressed here and there until he found the right button and the big screen lit up with a purplish glow. It wanted a pin number.

His first instinct was to try the number 1409, which represented the 14th of the 9th, the date of his and Chrissie's wedding anniversary. It would be twenty-five years next September and he'd already started thinking about special ways to celebrate; but that was before, before he realised that their marriage was becoming a sham. They invariably used those four digits as their pin numbers; it made it simple with so many cards and shared accounts.

He was disappointed but not surprised when it worked.

He leant on the bonnet of the Jaguar and fiddled with the phone. Chrissie hadn't put in any names to associate with the numbers but he recognized them all the same – there were only two numbers in there, and they were both Dewi's. Now he knew; now he had to accept what he had probably known subconsciously for some time, months perhaps. When he'd first found the mobile lying next to her handbag in the hall he'd thought of Dewi immediately because he'd pulled the same trick before, giving his current bit on the side a secret communication device. They'd even shared a few laughs about the audacity of it. 'My totline', is what Dewi had called it – his hotline to totty.

The anger started then.

The anger increased as he paced around the car waiting for one of Dewi's minions to show up; he walked towards the main road and stood on the corner watching the vehicles as they came into view and then drifted past leaving the tone of their engines and the redness of their rear lights like echoes on his brain. The road was busy so that a regular pattern developed and having nowhere to go, the anger changed gradually into a despair that got more intense with each passing vehicle.

A police car pulled over. Colin nodded at the driver; it was Carl, a nice safe local boy who had helped him out once or twice with awkward fares.

"What's going on Col?" Carl asked.

"Fucking car's broken down."

Carl laughed: "Not again."

"It's not funny."

"No, it's a shame, it's a nice motor. Hang on."

Carl turned the police car into Vauxhall and parked next to the Jaguar. He got out and did a circuit of the car waiting for Colin to catch up.

"Give me the keys."

Colin handed the keys to the policeman, who got into the driver's seat and turned them in the ignition. The bloody thing started straight away.

Carl got out smiling.

Colin shook his head. "Thanks, I owe you."

"Cars are like women, no point trying to work them out, just give them a gentle nudge now and again and talk to them softly."

Colin managed a quiet chuckle.

The policeman's radio interrupted their manly chat.

"Got to go, take care now."

Colin got back into the driver's seat of the XJ6 and waited, trying to compose himself. He still had the silver phone in his hand. He stared at it for a minute then flung it over his shoulder and onto the back seat. He couldn't move or think, he was empty of everything except a vague feeling of anger coated in a blanket of despair.

The inanity of *The Simpson's* tune brought him back to consciousness. He stared at the screen unable to make sense of the sequence of digits that it displayed. He flung that phone onto the back seat as well, put the car into drive and pressed the accelerator. He turned left into the dual carriageway without looking and drove full throttle towards the Thomas Arms. If he couldn't do anything about his mess of a life at least he could sort that arrogant bastard out. He wasn't going to let anyone else take the piss out of him; the town was too small for that, once you got labelled as a loser that was that, the small-minded bastards just ground you down. He had little left to lose and what he had wasn't worth keeping.

He parked the car haphazardly outside the pub and

walked in looking for blood. The greasy-haired shit was sitting at a table in the bar with half a dozen other meatheads, drinking and laughing. Colin pointed at him and shouted.

"You. Outside – now."

The man looked up at him, laughed and turned to his mates.

"That's the cab driver."

Then he stood up and moved towards Colin, stopping a couple of feet away from him, hands on hips defiantly.

"What's your problem?"

"You owe me. Hand it over."

"That's a joke, I should be suing you for shock, you couldn't drive a fucking golf ball. Wanker."

Colin's anger returned full force and he lunged at the man, grabbing him in a headlock and pushing him to the floor. He put his hands around the young man's neck and started squeezing and shaking. Then his sense of reality diminished, suddenly he was lost in a melee of random sounds, colours and sensations. He felt himself being lifted off the man on the floor, who was screaming for someone to call the cops.

Colin tore himself away from the unknown hands that were holding him and ran out of the pub, heart pounding. The anger had gone and he laughed to himself as he revved the old Jaguar up and drove away. He had no idea where he was going, but he knew one thing; he was finished with the town. It could keep the meagre rations it had doled out to him, it could keep the claustrophobic streets and pubs and Dewi could keep his discarded wife.

A few minutes later he parked the XJ6 outside the railway station, left the keys in the ignition and the two phones on the back seat, walked onto the platform and waited. It was 9 o'clock.

A train arrived two minutes later, god bless British Rail or whatever it was called now. He didn't know where he was going and he didn't care, he had a couple of hundred left on his credit card and he had the pin number to the joint account; that would do.

He sat down in an empty seat and looked around the carriage. There was an attractive woman sitting across the aisle, she looked up and smiled at him. He smiled back. Possibilities, he thought, at last there were possibilities. He was coming in to land.

Bees

Waking up from a seriously good dream, hearing the raucous sound of his mother's high-pitched voice, as she violently tore open the curtains of his bedroom, was not Darren's idea of fun. It was another warm sunny day and school beckoned. He wished he was eighteen like his brother Adam. Adam lounged around all day, getting up when he liked and staying awake until the early hours flicking the channels on the large flat television set.

Darren grunted bad-temperedly at his mother's entreaties, and snuggled harder into the warm comfort of the bedding, it had taken all night for it to mature to just the right degree of cosiness.

"Darren," she shouted, in a voice that almost lifted his body out of the bed, by the power of its command. "Darren, GET UP, you'll miss the bus. Your breakfast is on the table. It's twenty to eight."

It wasn't his mother's voice but the delicious aroma of fresh toast wafting up the stairs that eventually transported him from the bed.

Sitting at the breakfast table Darren felt his body tell him that he should go and use the toilet in the privacy of his own home before he left for the raw experience of school. He wasn't partial to spending much time in the humid stench of the lower school's boys' toilets. He was just halfway into his first year, a fragile green shoot susceptible to the taunts and jibes of his cruel elders.

Darren sat on the toilet, staring absently at his feet scraping the vinyl flooring beneath him. His body performed its function. He had opened the frosted bathroom window behind his head, to create an air freshening draught; he didn't want to suffer the coarse comments of his father. "What a stink, Darren, what rubbish have you been eating to make a smell like that?" He would say.

It was late spring and the birds and the bees were going frantically about their important business; keeping their respective species alive for another year.

There was an alarming buzz behind him; it dawned on him that the open window might allow some unwanted guests to stray into the bathroom, perhaps attracted by the odours. A particularly vicious insect might alight on his exposed backside and inflict its painful sting. When he was younger, and less wise, a bee had taken the liberty of stabbing his upper arm with a poisonous jab. Boy, had he screamed then, in pain and in protest. He knew he wouldn't, couldn't, scream; at 12 years old; but he could do without the chance to prove that he was as tough as the brilliant and athletic Simon 'Poncey' Perkins, who had snapped an arm on the rugby field and not shed a single tear.

Darren turned his neck around to observe the source of the buzz; keep your eyes on them, that was the trick. A large hostile bee had entered the open window – if teachers and parents could bottle the essence of that threatening buzz and call it up at will there would be no discipline problems at school; and the vile 'green things' would be the first thing to disappear from his dinner plate.

Darren's fear increased at an exponential rate, until he realised, that the bee, was desperately trying to get out, constantly bumping into the frosted glass. He reached back and took a toothbrush from the plastic shelf next to the toilet. Using it as an arm's length probe he shooed the bee out of the window and resumed his contemplative pose. He would have to hurry if he was to catch the school bus; if he missed it, he'd have to crawl back home and beg his sarcastic father for a lift.

Another buzz filled his ears. He was in a dilemma; closing the window would shut out the intrusive bees, but it would also block off the escape route for the embarrassing smells. Darren decided on a compromise. He closed the window until it rested open just enough to encourage the freshness of the spring air outside to interact with the stale air of the bathroom. The angle of the opening was reduced as far as he dared; he hoped that any stray bee that happened to be passing would be too stupid to squeeze itself through the gap.

The buzzing outside increased in pitch and intensity. His head swivelled like an owl's searching for prey as he tried to ensure an intruder didn't sneak in. He became distracted and failed to finish his business; giving up in frustration. He washed his hands, flushed the toilet, and approached the window cautiously; hoping that he'd have the opportunity to exact his revenge, and squash one or two of the annoying buzzers with the end of the toothbrush. He peered tentatively through the small gap and risked moving the window open another notch to get a better view. He was curious, wanting to discover what it was that had attracted the insects to that particular window. At first he thought it might be the saucer of dried flower petals that his mother had left in the bathroom to act as a natural air freshener. The petals had been enhanced with a strong sweet perfume that was released when he ran his fingers through them. The bees showed no interest in coming into the room, even through the open window, so, he discounted that idea. He looked more closely at the part of the window ledge that was exposed through the opening. He could see tiny red specks of life no larger than a pin head scurrying this way and that, on legs that were so small, he could only assume they existed. They were minuscule red spider mites. 'Ah,' he thought, 'the bees must eat the spider mites'. He made a mental note to bring the heavy ancient encyclopaedia down from the top bookshelf, blow the dust off and look up the facts on the diet of bees, or maybe he'd just google it.

Darren dared to open the window yet another notch to get a better view; he continued to stare in fascination at the comings and goings of the mites, as they hurried, in between the cracks of the concrete. He imagined he was a God, benevolently watching over his subjects on the surface of the planet below.

A bee landed on the ledge. Darren's face was only inches away from it; he was so close that he could clearly see its antennae, twitching, scanning the environment. He tried to keep a wary eye on the bee but was distracted for a split second, by the activities of the red mites, who carried on as if they knew nothing of the existence of the monstrous insect that had invaded their world. When he flicked his eyes back to the spot where the bee should have been, there was no sign of it; it was gone. The bee had disappeared, he was sure it hadn't flown away; he would have noticed such a dramatic action. Another bee buzzed noisily onto the window ledge. This time Darren was determined that he wouldn't even blink, for fear of missing the strange force that came and made bees vanish in an instant.

The bee walked purposefully towards the bottom of the wooden window frame. Darren leant over a fraction more to follow its path, it looked as if it intended to crawl up the frame and into the bathroom. Just when the insect should have begun its ascent it walked through a hole between the window frame and the concrete of the ledge, disappearing like the first one had done. Darren had seen where the dangerous insect had gone. He considered the implications: the bee had crawled into some breach in the defences of the house; for all he knew, there were thousands of the creatures nesting there, between the brickwork. The thought of that heaving insect city buzzing and breeding just inches beyond the apparently solid walls, sent a shiver down his spine.

On the inside of the window sill was a yellow plastic bottle, it contained a white dusting powder that his father used; the powder was designed to be puffed in between the toes; supposed to be a cure for athlete's foot. He had gleaned that fact during those long sojourns in the bathroom as his backside developed a red ring in the shape of the toilet seat. He often read the labels of the containers, the shampoos, talcum powders and aftershaves. According to the label, the white powder contained fungicide. He had a vague notion that fungicide might be deadly to insects, that's what gave him the idea.

He picked up the container of foot powder and decided he'd puff it into the gap beneath the window frame, to observe the effect it would have on the bees as they returned from their forays. He guessed they'd have been out visiting the local flower population, to return laden with nectar, laying it in their hive for conversion into the precious honey that their race depended on. Systematically he sprayed the powder along the length of the windowsill making sure he didn't inhale any. He'd been warned often enough by parents and teachers, not to inhale substances he knew nothing about. He closed the container, put it back into its place on the inner sill, and waited for another bee to show up, so that he could test the defences he'd built.

Darren noticed that the population of spider mites was becoming more active. He followed an individual mite with his eyes until his vision went out of focus, then lost it in the pitted surface of the concrete. He refocused his eyes and picked up the frenzied passages of other mites, one of the tiny creatures rushed along, its back covered in the white powder, like a saddled camel. It amused him to see the panic-stricken red spots. He looked more closely at the deadly dust that he'd deposited in their world. The powder that he'd sprayed looked like huge mounds of snow. Amongst the mounds, tiny red bodies struggled to free themselves like skiers trapped in a sudden avalanche.

A returning bee, alerted him of its presence by its tell-tale buzz. The bee landed on the concrete like its predecessors had, its antennae probing. It headed recklessly for the gap. It stopped short of the white hillocks and crawled up and down the length of the windowsill searching for an unblocked entrance to its city. Darren eyes focused like a microscope on the rear end of the bee; it was throbbing as if in anger or frustration. The sight alarmed him, he jerked his head back quickly, afraid of the threat that the throbbing communicated. He imagined the bee landing on his body and he visualised the pulsating abdomen jabbing its sting into his soft skin. The bee paused momentarily as if gathering its resources of inner strength, before deciding to take a chance with its life, then, it darted rapidly towards the opening. It blundered into the white powder and retreated at once confused and alarmed. The bee shook its head like a dog shaking off water to try and dislodge the powder that had been deposited on its tiny face. Darren could clearly see that face. Its expression showed complete disorientation from the effects of the powder, was he imagining it, or did he hear it snort a tiny sneeze? It was one of the funniest things he had ever seen, better than the bawdy wit of Alan Carr, better even than the sight of the brilliant and athletic Simon 'Poncey' Perkins, getting crushed on the rugby field.

Slowly his perception of the insect's predicament changed; it was no longer a cleverly designed miniature toy that had been manufactured specially for his amusement. Darren thought he could hear the bee screaming at the unseen God, who had cruelly separated it from its only purpose. The anger, frustration and pain that the bee felt were tangible. Shame made his head jerk away from the effects of his unthinking immature actions.

He looked again at the activities of the microscopic red spider mites. The mites were settling down, coming to terms with the disturbance; redefining their world after the catastrophe. His tiny red subjects knew nothing of his divine aspirations. He was not a God at all, he had wreaked havoc in their world; he was a terrible demon. His only creation had been a disaster; how could he know what they felt? What were their motives? What right had he to alter their environment in so drastic a way? What could he do to mitigate the calamity that he had created?

Two more bees arrived from the heavens and hovered uncertainly above the ledge, like helicopter gunships, facing the window. They did not venture to land on the sill, like their foolhardy brother. The powdered insect was still wandering about in confusion, shaking itself; it was as if it was warning them of the dire effects of the evil white dust. On their faces, he could see the resignation of defeat. They had only wanted to execute the duty that they'd been given the gift of life to perform. The tragedy had robbed them of the purpose of their short existence. A great sadness fleetingly occupied Darren's young heart and he experienced the pain of guilt.

He was shaken from the sad flow of ideas that signalled the beginning of the end of childhood innocence by the hysterical sound of his mother's voice, calling from downstairs. "Darren, what are you doing in there? Come on and finish your breakfast. It's getting late. You'll miss the school bus."

Darren snapped out of the trance he'd been in, carefully closed the window and rushed downstairs. He hated missing the bus. All thoughts of bees and mites evaporated from his mind as he leapt down the stairs and into another school day. He carefully brushed his hair and adjusted his tie in the hall mirror. He cursed to himself as he tied the laces of his black leather shoes, cursed at his mother when he discovered his rugby kit missing from his school bag. Finally he gulped down the dregs of the milky tea grabbed the last of his breakfast from the bone china plate and ran for the bus munching the wholemeal toast covered in thick sweet honey.

Noodles

Part One

It's always later. Here's a thing you may not know —
smoking tobacco doesn't always kill you, nor does
crossing the road, nor flying a kite. The world is mad.
The trouble is the more you think about it and the
more sense you try to make of it all, the less sense it
makes and the less sure you are. I wish I'd never
started, but there you go, I've opened the box.

It all began some 15 years ago when I was still a
young man.

I first saw her in my shop. She came in looking for
noodles. We didn't sell noodles, they weren't so
popular then — at least not in this part of the Western
hemisphere. I looked up, I was weighing black-eyed
beans at the time, 500 grams poured into a crinkly
cellophane bag, sealed with sellotape and festooned
with a hand-scrawled sticky label.

She didn't come in at first, just pushed the door
open and raised her voice:

"Noodles?"

I half looked up, afraid of screwing the sellotape
up: "Sorry," I said. "We don't do noodles."

"That's interesting," she said, walking into the shop
and towards me at the counter.

I looked up all the way then, and into her eyes.

Wow!

"We've got some whole wheat pasta."

"No, that's all right thanks. That packaging is
interesting."

"Oh yeah."

"Yes – very crisp, very natural. Do you mind if I have a closer look?"

"Carry on."

She grabbed a bundle of empty cellophane bags and rubbed them between her hands. She was as attractive as a woman can be; perfect dark-gold skin, long brunette hair and brown eyes that delivered nothing but beauty.

"I'm a packaging designer," she said. "Cellophane I guess?"

"Yeah, they're more biodegradable than plastic; they're lovely to handle. Kind of natural."

"They're beautiful," she said, dropping the bags delicately on the counter, like she was giving freedom to a fallen fledgling.

I nodded.

"So, you don't do noodles," she said, shaking her head. "I'll call again."

She was gone.

That's the thing about running a shop, especially a busy shop, and you have to be busy when you're selling individual items like 500 grams of black-eyed beans for a quid a pop. It takes a mountain of quids to keep a life going I can tell you. The thing is that you get to deal with a lot of people on a one-to-one basis, sometimes hundreds in a day, and when you've been at it for a number of years that's a big bunch of people. Thousands of variations of the human face imprinted in the eaves of your brain, thousands of whining voices asking the same stupid questions: *What's the difference between a Fava Bean and a*

Broad Bean? Or *Do you sell cod liver oil capsules?* Or *would you like to give me a bucket of money to put your business's name in a small box in the local paper?* I should have made an FAQ for wholefood shopkeepers and glued it to the window.

You'd think that when you've come eye-to-eye with tens of thousands of human beings no-one should be able to get access to your serotonin store merely by looking at you, but they can and they do. Are they magicians? Are they angels? Are they aliens? Maybe it's just me. Maybe, I thought, maybe it's something to do with matching genes. The little blighters are communicating, or trying to communicate through our very eyes. Maybe I was a deluded twat and all she saw was a shabby shopkeeper.

Anyway, she was gone and the full-frontal lobe of my brain was imprinted. I fucked up the black-eyed beans, poured nearly a whole kilo all over the floor of the shop; I swept half of them under the shelves — they'd keep.

Must have been two or three weeks before I saw her again.

* * *

That night, the night after the day of the noodle incident, I went to the pub with two of my housemates, Bill and Phil. We had this posh pub round the corner that hardly anyone went to, especially on week nights. I don't know why, it was a nice pub and the beer was always well-kept, so we had formed a habit of going there three, sometimes four times a week between Sunday and Thursday. A middle-aged gay couple ran the pub, well I say middle-aged but Col was about forty and Gavin was maybe ten years younger. They seemed middle-aged to me because they were so straight, obviously not straight in the gay sense, but you know what I mean.

Bill had a theory about life: "It's like a journey," he said. "And you can make a journey easy by planning everything meticulously, that way you can avoid most of the dangers that inevitably come with journeys."

Phil disagreed: "It's not a journey, you wouldn't call falling off a cliff a journey, that's what life is like – once your body is in the air you have no control – yeah you can flap around and scream a bit, but sure as eggs is eggs, you're going to hit the bottom according to the rules of gravity."

I swayed between the two theories: "Yes," I'd say, "Life is like falling off a cliff but you can grow wings, only little wings, but enough to fight with, and that's what it's all about – it's a fight between chaos and order, it's got to be that way, otherwise there would be no life."

That night we were all a bit subdued. Seeing that girl in the shop had kicked something off in me, feelings of loss, of what could have been, but also feelings of hope for what could still be. There I was just a year or so off thirty and still as single as a panda in a zoo.

"Hey boys," I said. "How's about we do something different tonight?"

"What do you mean, different?" Bill asked suspiciously.

"You know, let's go into town or something, maybe go to a club, or even grab a curry."

"I wish I could," Phil said, "but you know I'm skint, I don't even know how I'm going to pay next month's rent."

"My shout," I said. "I owe you one I'm sure."

Bill's suspicions seemed satisfied by that. "Yeah, I'm up for it, not the club though, just a curry. I could do with cheering up, I had a nasty setback today."

"What's that?" I asked.

"I didn't get that job."

"That's tough."

"Yes, ah well," he sighed, "just have to try harder next time. I'm sure I can put up with the insurance office for a bit longer."

We had a couple of pints, which I paid for, and walked up Station Road and into town. It was about nine o'clock, a dry still evening in mid-October. As we passed Aldo's caff we heard raised voices. Aldo was a proud Italian man in his early fifties, I'd been in school with his nephew Tony, so naturally I stopped and looked in.

Bill held back at the edge of the pavement and Phil just carried on walking, but only because he was trundling along in his woe-ridden parallel universe of unemployment and overdue bills.

I pushed the door inwards and saw Aldo and an old woman screaming at each other, his hands clenched tightly on the shoulders of her heavy, dirty coat. I recognised her as one of the bums that haunted the town and made fragrant menopausal women cringe with embarrassment; a week or so earlier I'd seen her harangue a newsagent on Station Road until he caved in and gave her a pack of ten Lambert and Butler's, but only until she won on the Bingo – she promised.

"Oi!" I shouted.

Aldo seemed startled by my presence and looked up; then he looked at me with a lost, pleading expression as if he had suddenly become completely bewildered by the world he found himself in. He must have relaxed his grip a bit, because the old bag lady pulled herself free, pushed past me and out of the shop, leaving the stink of fresh piss in her wake.

I looked again at Aldo, he staggered backwards against the espresso machine and moved his hands to his stomach. His brilliant white apron was stained with red.

I heard Bill's voice behind me: "What's going on Pete? What's happening?"

I moved quickly over to Aldo and helped him to a seat at one of tables in the café.

"Keep still," I told him. "We'll get an ambulance, just hang on."

Aldo stared at me, his mouth hanging loose in an expression of incredulity. His eyes closed and he slumped forwards on to the table. I tried to shake him but he was a dead weight.

"Is he all right?" Bill asked nervously. "I'll call an ambulance."

By the time the police and ambulance arrived, Phil had found his way back – he'd walked all the way to the restaurant at the other side of town before realising he was on his own.

I'd been in a few cop-shops before that, but never as a respected member of the public who had witnessed a madwoman stab a café owner with a pastry fork. Aldo was all right; he had some nasty cuts on his stomach and a bit of torn skin on his forehead from when he'd fainted on the table and nutted the sugar-pourer, but otherwise he was as bolshie as ever.

It was a few days later and I'd popped in to see him in the café on the way to the police station.

"As long as I never see the old bag again, I don't care what happens to her," he said.

***

Part Two

"Thanks for coming in again, just wanted to check a couple of things." The detective was typical, a tall, plump Welsh boy with shiny black shoes. I chuckled to myself, imagining him trying to be inconspicuous in a field full of e'd up munters.

"Like I said, when I went into the café, it had already happened – just a lot of noise and confusion and then Aldo's blood."

"Silly bugger, doesn't want a fuss."

"Yeah, he told me, I think he's ashamed."

"Just as well I suppose, anyway, it's best left to Social Services to deal with bums like her. They're more trouble than they're worth. You know, some people just don't know how to live; they don't know what life is about – making things difficult for ordinary people like us."

"I guess so."

What a dull young hambone he was.

Thing is, the next time I saw her, the noodle woman, she was with him! Him! the dozy detective. She smiled at me as I walked into the pub; he raised his eyebrows in recognition as well. They exchanged whispers and knowing nods. I had to have a shot of brandy before my pint to come to terms with it. Bill was with me; we had decided not to bother asking Phil, he hadn't come home by the time we went out and he was such a moaning bastard. Mind you, it would have been nice to have another body available to share the dull thump of Bill's wanky philosophy.

Anyway, this was the late nineties, long after Maggie Thatcher's destructive decade when she took on the guise of the god Shiva and dismantled society, pit-prop by pit-prop. Nobody really cared about anything other than their own arses – but why him? Why would an intensely intelligent and beautiful woman end up with a tosspot like him?

I couldn't stop myself from looking over at her every time I raised the glass to my lips and in most of the seconds in between. They seemed relaxed together; perhaps I was wrong about him. Then, another young buck with shiny shoes came into the pub and sat down next to the noodle girl and the copper. They spoke earnestly for a few seconds and then the two policemen left in a hurry. The noodle girl stood up and started to put her coat on.

Now, I'm like most people when an impulse to do something out of the box wells up in my chest – I fight it and tell myself to get a grip, but then, maybe because she was such a sparkly diamond of a woman and well worth the risk, the impulse overcame my social conditioning. It's a bit vague but by the time my logical, doubting, nagging brain kicked in, it was too late. I was already standing eye-to-eye with her and halfway through a feeble introduction.

" . . . . noodles, you wanted noodles, I just wanted to say, we've got noodles now."

She laughed insincerely and smiled politely. It hurt me; then I saw the pain in her eyes and forgave her. I gave her a big smile, feeling protective towards her, seeing her pain and wanting to shoo it all away.

She relaxed then and the other part of her, the perfect feminine beauty I'd previewed in the shop, took over.

"Yes, I remember," she said. "Thanks, I'll call in."

"Yeah – anytime," I said.

We let each other fall back into our own realities.

I sighed; I'd had another fix, enough for now.

His name was Sal

He was an American, a couple of years older than me. I was sixteen.

In the summer of 1968, I hitched from my dreary Welsh town to see Pink Floyd in Hyde Park. After a long, scary, but interesting journey, involving a lift in an abused Transit with a stoned roadie, I arrived in the park after midnight the night before the concert and leaned against a tree to rest and absorb the vibes. Excited fellow travellers buzzed around me looking for somewhere safe to crash. Despite my exhaustion I felt I was part of something significant, a revolution was taking place and I was at the heart of it.

A pair of London louts tried to sell me a lump of dodgy-looking dope, it was probably chewing tobacco, or henna, or something. They looked shifty and vicious, like sly hyenas. I felt exposed and alone, so I shook my head and turned my back on them. I was skint anyway. The big one pushed me against the tree and pulled a knife. A young man in a black leather jacket stopped and stared narrowly at them. His hair was slicked back like James Dean, his face smooth and unreadable. The dealers sized him up, thought the better of it, and swaggered away into the gloom.

That's how I met Sal.

Sal had survived the streets of LA, and wasn't afraid of Hyde Park lowlifes. He'd lived on his finely-tuned wits, trekked solo all over America, all over the world. He'd wielded bigger knives, and guns, real guns, with real bullets. He wasn't on the run as such, just travelling to take the heat out of things. We stayed together that night, huddled at the foot of that tree, smoking joints that Sal rolled from his own stash of Mexican grass. The next day we cruised through the crowds, the music a mere background to our conversation – the gathering of colourful humanity its wallpaper. Sal returned with me to my town in the sticks, to lie low, he said, though I didn't really know who he was hiding from, or why.

There was something about Sal I recognised immediately, something real – he was the most palpably true person I'd ever met. We were best friends instantly. He became more of a brother to me than my real brothers. We were as close to each other as it was possible for either of us to be close to anyone. He found a cheap room and hung around for a few months, working the night shift in a bakery for cash to pay the rent. He was still there at Christmas.

A skinny freckled Scottish girl, Sandy, had blagged some Ephedrine from a pharmacy – it was easier to do that then. She told us she'd made up some story about asthma and was given a batch of the small white pills, although I think she really was severely asthmatic, if the way she struggled for breath was anything to go by. She'd also procured several bottles of a cough medicine laced with morphine, and more than a few packs of travel sickness pills that contained hyoscine, an anaesthetic drug. A Christmas treat, she said.

I went out after lunch and walked into town. I didn't like to think of Sal alone on Christmas Day in his tiny bedsit, in a place he barely knew that didn't understand him. We sat on the edge of his bed and smoked a joint. He told me about his brother, in prison in California, for murder, but he was innocent, Sal said. He'd been framed by the cops and the feds, and one day Sal was going to prove it. I believed him.

Sal was agitated, constantly pausing to listen to some real or imagined threat, or peering through the grubby net curtains into the empty street below.

"What's up Sal?" I asked.

"Nada," he said. "It's all cool. Come on man, let's split, let's go find some action."

We slid around the deserted streets and spotted Sandy slumped in the doorway outside Woolworths. She looked tired and dejected. We decamped to the park and occupied a bench overlooking the football field. Sandy shared the Ephedrine with us. We got excitable and animated. There was a large pond at the other end of the field; we bounced across the thawing grass and picked our way through the snow-patched reeds around the water, smoking joints of Lebanese Red until we tired of our heavy sodden shoes. We squelched back across the field. Sandy babbled about the hard gangs of Glasgow. Sal perched on the edge of the bench, nodding rapidly. I said I'd better get home, my family would be wondering where I'd got to, on Christmas Day.

I was almost delirious with the drugs when I got back in but the rest of my family were too drunk to notice, or to care. My mother was drinking sherry and staring blankly at the television without taking it in. She deserved it, after all the work she'd put into preparing the meal, and into generally looking after the family, as she often reminded us. My father was slumped in his chair, snoring, a half drunk glass of beer still clamped in his hand. He worked long enough and hard enough the rest of the year so that we could afford stuff like Christmas so I suppose it was his due. My brother Ken, even though he was only fourteen, was also drunk and lying on his bed upstairs, groaning. He deserved that too. My older brother Tom was out, as usual, probably sniffing around after the Johnson sisters in the top site.

There wasn't any edible dinner left over so I stole half of the large fruit cake that was sitting untouched on the sideboard, it would never get eaten anyway; it never was, unless it was forced on reluctant visitors, already over-stuffed with their own Christmas.

I helped myself to a pint bottle of bitter from the slab in the pantry and gulped it on a slow walk back to town to catch up with Sal and Sandy. It hadn't been much of a Christmas for them so far. Sandy was still in the park, bouncing on the bench, rambling obsessively about corrupt police and crazy American bastards. She ignored me when I asked her where Sal was, just kept on ranting, her eyes bulging like a maniac. I gave her a hunk of cake. She stared at it with a puzzled look and put it on the bench next to her. She handed me a bottle of cough medicine. I glugged half of it against the best efforts of my stomach to puke it up – it would be worth it when the morphine kicked in. I tapped a clutch of the travel sickness pills into the palm of my hand, threw them into my mouth, and washed them down with another slug of the cough medicine.

Sal wasn't in his bedsit so I started the walk home. The drugs kicked in, the world dissolved, and I thought it best, despite the stupor my family was in, to head back to the park instead, and wait until I came down. Sandy had gone, the cake was still on the bench, untouched, maybe the ducks would appreciate it. I stuttered through the melting snow across the sodden field towards the pond.

There was a body lying face down at the water's edge – it was Sal.

His nose and mouth were in the water. I pulled his hair to lift his head and pushed him onto his back, he was heavy – a dead weight. It wasn't Sal anymore; it was a pale corpse, already cold. I retched.

I prayed that when the retching stopped I would be completely straight and there would be no Sal lying dead at the edge of a pond in a small Welsh town. I prayed that we would be back in Hyde Park again, lying on the grass, leaning on our elbows in the sun, listening to Pink Floyd and staring down villainous drug dealers. But when I stopped it was still real. It was still Christmas Day, and Sal was still dead.

A black Labrador snuffled up to Sal's body. I looked around. The dog's owner was standing a few feet away, a small fat man in his fifties, his mouth open in shock. I shook my head and shrugged at him.

"Here boy," he called to his dog.

The dog trotted back to its master.

The man looked afraid. "What happened?" he asked.

"I just found him. I don't know."

"Wait there," the man said. "I'll get someone."

I was alone with the dead body of the best friend I'd ever had and I'd taken too many of the wrong kind of drugs, so I wasn't surprised when I saw a group of shadowy figures emerge from the water like ghouls in the mist, and glide towards me muttering murder with American accents. I covered my ears with my hands and squeezed my eyes shut tightly. I knew I could dissolve that nightmare but I also knew the real nightmare was lying next to me on the damp banks of the pond.

The police arrived in a surge of noise – someone was shaking me, saying, "He's in shock."

I was taken to hospital and put in a quiet room to recover. A police detective came to see me. He asked me who I was and he asked me what drugs I'd taken. I told him my name and address but not about the drugs – nor about Sandy. He didn't seem to mind.

Nothing happened for two weeks. Sandy disappeared, I never saw her again. Sal's sister came over from America to claim his body. The police gave her my address and she called to see me before she left. She wanted to know how her brother had spent the last days of his life.

She told me that Sal had always been a troubled and troublesome child. His parents had disowned him and sent him over the pond to live with his aunt in Bristol just to get him out of their sight. He went AWOL from his aunt's after a few weeks and they hadn't heard from him since. As far as she knew, he'd never been involved in any gangs or with any guns. He didn't have a brother. His name wasn't even Sal; that was just a name he'd taken from a book. His real name was Jack.

It wasn't a knife or a bullet; it wasn't the gangs of

LA, or Glasgow. In the end, what brought Sal down was the poison inside himself, intensified by a cruel world and weak parents. For all his bravado and bluster, Sal was just a lost little boy who needed love.

He may have been a loser called Jack to his family, but he'll always be Sal to me, and forty-odd years later, he's still the best and truest friend I've ever had.

****

www.ingramcontent.com/pod-product-compliance
Lightning Source LLC
Chambersburg PA
CBHW030623130626
46552CB00002B/693